SPURIOUS

SPURIOUS

Lars Iyer

MELVILLEHOUSE
BROOKLYN, NEW YORK

First Melville House Printing: December 2010

Melville House Publishing
145 Plymouth Street
Brooklyn, New York 11201
mhpbooks.com

ISBN: 978-1-935554-28-8

Printed in the United States of America

1 2 3 4 5 6 7 8 9 10

Library of Congress Cataloging-in-Publication Data

Iyer, Lars.
  Spurious : a novel / Lars Iyer.
    p. cm.
  ISBN 978-1-935554-28-8
  I. Title.
  PR6109.Y47S78 2011
  823'.92--dc22

                                          2010038113

To Sinéad

I'm a terrible influence on W., everyone says that. Why does he hang out with me? What's in it for him? The great and the good are shaking their heads. Sometimes W. goes back to the high table and explains himself. I am something to explain, W. says. He has to account for me to everyone. Why is that?

I don't feel I have to account for myself, W. says, that's what it is. I've no real sense of shame. It must be something to do with my Hinduism, W. muses. —'You're an ancient people, but an innocent one, unburdened by shame', W. says. On the other hand, it could be simply due to my stupidity. I'm freer than him, W. acknowledges, but more stupid. It's an innocent kind of stupidity, but it's stupidity nonetheless.

It's been my great role in his life, W. says, helping him escape the high table. He's down among the low tables now, he says, in the chimps' enclosure.

W. remembers when I was up and coming, he tells me. He remembers the questions I used to ask, and how they would resound beneath the vaulted ceilings. —'You seemed so intelligent then', he says. I shrug. 'But when any of us read your work . . .', he says, without finishing the sentence.

So was he ever up and coming?, I ask W. He was, he remembers. That was a golden age. Everyone looked up to him. Everything was expected of him! Each morning, he got up and read and took notes until he went to bed. He had a desk and a bed in his room, and his books and his notebooks, but nothing else. He didn't go out, didn't drink, but just read and took notes, day after day. What went wrong? —'Drinking', he says. 'I drank too much, I smoked too much'. Why did he drink? —'The sense of the apocalypse', W. says. 'That it was all for nothing'.

W. is impressed by my stammer. —'You stammer and stutter', says W., 'and you swallow half your words. What's wrong with you?' Every time I see him, he says, it gets a little worse. The simplest words are beginning to defeat me, W. says. Maybe it's mini-strokes, W. speculates. That would account for it. —'You had one just there, didn't you?'

Perhaps, W. muses, my stammering and stuttering is a sign of shame. W. says he never really thought I was capable of it, shame, but perhaps it's there nonetheless. —'Something inside you knows you talk rubbish', he says. 'Something knows the unending bilge that comes out of your mouth'.

'Something inside you always knew, didn't it?', W. says. 'Didn't your teachers say as much on your report card: *Lars has a stutter, but it doesn't seem to bother him*'? But why was I unbothered?, W. wonders. Did I imagine that my shame should end with the *sign* of my shame? I wasn't *ashamed of my shame*, that's the point, W. says. My shame didn't prompt me to thought and reflection. It didn't make me change my ways.

It's all down to my non-Catholicism and non-Judaism, W. says. Only for a Jew and a Catholic like himself (W.'s family are converts), is it possible to feel shame *about* shame.

W. dreams of serious conversation. Not that it would have serious topics, you understand, he says—that it would be concerned, for example, with the great topics of the day. —'Speech *itself* would be serious', he says with great vehemence. That's what he's found with the real thinkers he's known. Everything they say is serious; they're incapable of being *un*serious.

Even I become serious when a real thinker is about, W.'s observed. We remember that afternoon in Greenwich when W. was lost in conversation with one such thinker. I was leaning in, trying to listen; I had a sense of the seriousness of the conversation, W. could see it. He was impressed; for once I wasn't going to ruin it by talking about blowholes or something.

'Conversation!', exclaims W. That's what friendship's all about. He thinks even I have a sense of that. —'It's why you stammer', says W. 'It's why you swallow half of your words'.

'When did you know?', W. says with great insistence. 'When did you know you weren't going to amount to anything? *Did* you know?', he asks, because sometimes he suspects I never did. Well *he* knows, at any rate, for both of us. —'Neither of us is going to amount to anything!', he says with finality. 'Neither of us! Anything!'

W. speaks mournfully about my intellectual decline. Of course it's not my decline he laments, but that of his own judgement, and his own fantastic hopes: how was it that he placed them in me? Why did he need to place them in anyone at all?

How's it come to this?, W. says. What wrong turn did he make? He was like Dante, he says, lost in a dark forest.

—'And there you were', he says, 'the idiot in the forest'. I was always lost, wasn't I? I didn't even know I was lost, but I was lost. Or perhaps I was never lost. Perhaps I belonged in the forest, W. muses. Perhaps I am only that forest where W. is wandering, he says, he's not sure.

'Do you think it's possible to die of stupidity?' W. sighs. 'Not as a consequence of that stupidity', he notes, 'but *from* stupidity. And shame', W. asks me, 'do you think you could die of shame, I mean literally die?'

We should hang ourselves immediately, W. thinks, it's the only honourable course of action. We are compromised, utterly compromised.

Things are bad. We should kill ourselves, W. says. He's thought of setting himself on fire before a crowd like that madman in Tarkovsky's film. —'Not that it would do any good', he says.

Early morning at the airport. —'Beer', W. commands. 'You can pay for this'.

We're always renewed, W. says., when we set off once again to speak in Europe. Always young and uncowed, full of fresh hope and new happiness, toasting each other in foreign countries and falling down drunk in foreign gutters. Are we really that shameless?, W. wonders. But perhaps it doesn't matter whether we're shameless or not: we'll do exactly the same thing anyway and will be eternally surprised at the rediscovery of our own idiocy.

But are we really that innocent?, W. wonders. Don't we, at one level or another, *know* our own idiocy? Doesn't it saturate our awareness to the extent that we know nothing else? But by some miracle, we always regain just enough innocence, just enough forgetting for it all to begin again.

'What have I told you!', says W. as we board the train in Frankfurt. 'This is public space. Pub-lic. That means outside your head'. He points to my head. 'Private'. And then out to the world. 'Public'.

W. is a great upholder of this division. Abolish the public/private divide and you abolish civilisation, W. always says. He looks around him contentedly. —'See how quiet it is in Europe? It's civilised', he says, 'not like you'.

Europe makes him gentler, better, W. says. It improves him. It's the public spaces, he says. They're so quiet in Germany. So calm.

Later, and W. is in a contemplative mood. Is he thinking of his Canadian boyhood? No, W. is thinking of his many European trips. He's been back and forth across Europe, back and forth . . . W.'s travelled. Not like me. —'You haven't been anywhere. It's obvious'.

W. is an experienced traveller. Take drinking, for example. He can pace himself, he says. Morning to night, he drinks like a European. Steadily. That's the secret. You should watch the Poles, he says, they're experts. *Poles—experts*, I write down in my notebook.

The best train journey, we remember, was the long one from Warsaw to Wrocław. Small round tables like in a cafe, but in the dining carriage of a train. And waiter service—discrete, attentive, but not servile. We drank, steadily. Europe passed by the window, flat and green. All was well: our guide was with us, we felt secure, safe; like small children with their parents, we had nothing to fear.

This time, we have to look after ourselves. Of course, it's already gone wrong. We steel ourselves: we have to concentrate. Are we on the right train? Is it going in the right direction? Left to fend for ourselves, we become panicky. Then the conductor comes round to take our tickets. *Alles klar*, he says, in a voice that is infinitely calm. It soothes us. *Alles klar,* I write in my notebook: we're in safe hands, this is a safe country. Over the next few days, we will only have to repeat his phrase to feel secure; it watches over us like a guardian angel.

I remind W. of his photo album. Photos of the young W., happy in Canada, with his family, who are likewise happy, and then photos of W. in England. The fall, W. calls it. The move, says W., that's when the disaster happened. His parents brought them back to England, to Wolverhampton, of all places. —'Wolverhampton!' says W., 'can you imagine!' Ah, what he might have been, had he stayed in Canada!, he sighs.

W. is lost in a Canadian reverie. They had a dog which was half wolf, he tells me, and she would follow him on his paper round, leading him by the arm. —'She took my hand in her mouth and led me, it was amazing. She never barked. And when we left, she starved herself to death, because she missed us so much. That's loyalty'.

Above all, W. admires loyalty. Sal's loyal, he says.

She's loyalty itself, just as he is. You're not loyal, W. always insists. You'd break the phalanx. You'd betray me—for a woman. He insists on this. When have I betrayed him in the past? —'You will betray me', says W., 'I'm certain of it'.

Canada. Betrayed, I write in my notebook.

Kafka's our spiritual leader, W. and I agree over cocktails in the Münsterplatz. He's gone the furthest, we agree. But we need more immediate leaders, too. W.: 'We're stupid, we need to be led'. Didn't we long ago decide we could redeem ourselves only by creating opportunities for those more capable than ourselves? —'It's our gift', says W., 'we know we're stupid, but we also know what stupidity is not'.

We ought to throw ourselves at their feet and ask them to forgive us. We always stop short of this, of course. We have to remember not to tell them, each of them, that they are our new leader. It would only frighten them off, W. says. No one should ever know he or she is our leader, we agree. Only we should know. And we should follow them in secret.

In truth, we have found several leaders. Our *first* leader was always an example to W. and me. —'I'm not very interesting', he always insisted, 'but my . . . thoughts are interesting'. *My . . . thoughts*! We were particularly impressed by the *way* he said it. *My . . . thoughts* . . . It was as though there were an infinite distance between those words. As though he had nothing to do with his thoughts! As though they had him and not the other way round! He felt a kind of *moral duty* to his thoughts, we remember. It was as though his life was only a receptacle for something infinitely more important.

'He was completely serious', W. remembers, 'not like us'. Completely serious! And there was a kind of *lightness* in that seriousness, he remembers, as though thinking were a kind of beatitude. What will we ever know of the infinite lightness of thought? W. wonders. Of thought's laughter, which laughs in the eyes of the thinker touched with thought?

But then the disaster happened, W. remembers. We told him, didn't we? We told him he was our leader. We told him what we hoped he'd make us become. We told him of our hopes and fears . . . That's where it all went wrong, we agree. We scared him off. After that, we resolved never to tell our leaders that they were our leaders, but we couldn't help it.

Didn't the same thing happen with our *second* leader? Ah, our second leader! He had an absolute lucidity when he spoke of the interlacing of his life and thought, we agree. It was like looking into the clearest of rivers, W. says. How frankly and absolutely he spoke of his thoughts, and to anyone who asked! Frankly and absolutely, as though life were a glass to look through and not to live! Or that life was lived at another level, where thinking, real thought, was possible! —'A level of which we have no conception', says W.

But it happened again. 'Which one of us blurted it out', W. asks, 'you or me?' Regardless, the spell was broken. We had spoken to him of what we lacked and what he had. We spoke of cosmogony and the opposite of cosmogony, of the beginning of times and of their coming end . . .

Then there was the *third* leader. —'Ah, our third leader',

W. exclaims, 'the greatest one of all'.

Everyone knows to keep quiet when he speaks, W. says. He speaks very quietly himself, and is immensely modest, but everyone knows it: here is a thinker, here is thought in person. He lives in a different way from everyone else, that much is clear. He lives another kind of life, and his quietness is a sign of his elevation.

It's what everyone in the room knows when he speaks: he's better than the rest of us, cleverer; he occupies the stratosphere of pure thought. Thought is here, and we are touched by a cold and fiery hand, by what it would be impossible for us to think by ourselves. To have a thought that would burn our lives away like dross! To have the whole of our lives become clear and still like pools of water in northern forests!

We lean in, listening. He speaks so quietly, and we must be more quiet than we can be to hear. And for a moment, we forget we are apes, and listen with the whole of our being.

And then it happened again. We told him all we wanted was a leader and to be led by a leader. We told him about our first leader and our second leader, and our desertion by our first leader and our second leader. We told him of the *tohu vavohu* that comes at the beginning and will return at the end. We told him of the apocalypse and of waiting for the Messiah . . .

Will we find our new leader in Freiburg? It's unlikely, we agree as we sip our piña coladas.

Wandering back to the hotel, we lose ourselves in the streets, chancing upon the same section of waterway again and again, the same weir. The city's closing itself against us, we decide. Against the likes of us. It doesn't want us here. Should we throw ourselves in the river? Is that what it's telling us?

Kafka was always our model, we agree. How is it possible that a human being could write like that?, W. says, again and again. It's always at the end of the night when he says this, after we've drunk a great deal and the sky opens above us, and it is possible to speak of what is most important.

At the same time, we have Kafka to blame for everything. Our lives each took a wrong turn when we opened *The Castle*. It was quite fatal: there was literature itself! We were finished. What could we do, simple apes, but exhaust ourselves in imitation? We had been struck by something we could not understand. It was above us, beyond us, and we were not of its order.

Literature softened our brains, says W. —'We should have been doing maths. If we knew maths, we might amount to something. As it is, we'll amount to nothing'.

There's nothing wrong with literature per se, says W., who cannot go a day without speaking of Kafka, but it's had a bad effect on us. Besides, he says, he bets Kafka was good at maths. He was good at law, after all, which is probably a bit like maths. Perhaps we should drop out and become lawyers. Perhaps that would be the making of us.

Literature destroyed us: we've always been agreed on that. The *literary temptation* was fatal. Of course, it would be different if we read literature alongside philosophy, W. says, but literature, for us, could not help infecting our philosophy.

But doesn't W. admire the fact that we *feel* something about literature? Doesn't he think it's what saves us? W. is not persuaded. —'It makes us vague and full of pathos. That's all we have—pathos'.

Once, W. thought of himself as a writer, a literary writer. He filled notebook after notebook. It was in his early twenties. Everyone wants to be a literary writer in their early twenties, W. says. Of course no one ever is. W. realised it pretty quickly. He knew he was no Kafka, he says. That's what I don't know yet—I don't know I'm not Kafka. I don't have a sense of myself as a failure, which is ironic because I *am* a failure.

It would be different if either of us had literary talent, W. says. Do I think I have literary talent?, he asks me. W. *knows* he doesn't have literary talent, he says. But he doesn't think *I* know. Admittedly, I never said I had literary talent. But I don't deny it enough. Anyway, it's very clear: I don't have literary talent, W. says. And just so I know, I haven't got any philosophical talent either, he says. Does he have any philosophical talent? He has more than I do, he says. Just a little bit more, but that's already something.

His IQ's higher than mine, W. says. Just a little bit, but that's what separates us, man from ape. And he's from a higher class than me, W. says. —'I have manners. You have no manners. And you're continually touching yourself. Look at you: you're doing it now!' I take my hand out of my shirt. —'Why do you like touching your chest so much? Does it arouse you? Keep your hands on the table where I can see them. Read your book'.

For a long time, W. thought he might *become* Kafka. He was all W. read. Constantly, again and again, everything by him and everything about him, and he speaks lovingly of discovering the brightly coloured Schocken editions of Kafka.

It was one of those old Victorian libraries, he says, such as could be found in the towns and cities of the West Midlands. He probably hadn't read all the books in the children's section, he says, but there was nothing left that seemed worth reading. He asked a librarian for a ticket for the adult section of the library and, even though he was relatively young (he imagines himself being twelve or thirteen, but he was probably older), they allowed him one.

It was the brightness of the dust jackets that drew him in, W. says. They were fluorescent orange, he said, a bright and baffling colour. And when he opened the book, it was as if he had crossed over a threshold, as though there were another light streaming from its pages, a splendour that has fascinated him ever since.

For a long time, W. says, he saw little difference between Kafka and himself. Imagine it—a boy from Wolverhampton who thought he was a Jew from Prague! How is it possible for a human being to write like that?: yes, that was always W.'s question before Kafka.

How was it possible? W. stopped writing after his undergraduate years. He'd write all the time, but he realised he would never be Kafka. W. gave his notebooks and writings to a girlfriend. —'I didn't keep a scrap', he says, as German teenagers gather round us in the Augustinerplatz, playing early Depeche Mode on a ghetto blaster.

In the shops in Freiburg, they wipe the door handles after we leave and rearrange the books we looked at. What is it about us? Are we that disgusting?

We wanted to gaze at the great editions. At the collected works of Schelling, published by Vorlesung. At those of Nietzsche, edited by Colli and Montinari. W. wanted to look for Cohen's books, which are out of print in several languages. But the shop assistants were suspicious. Our German was deficient. Our questions went awry.

Tired of the city, we catch the train to Titisee and hire a pedallo to paddle out onto the lake. Feet on the dashboard, the blue bowl of the sky above us, we discuss the fate of Max Brod, who spent all his life writing commentaries and exegeses of Kafka's work, and the fate of Kafka, which seems altogether more dark and mysterious precisely because of Brod's commentaries and exegeses.

We discuss the inadequacy of political thought in tackling the question of political economy, and the failure of philosophical thought to pose, really pose, the question of *what matters most* . . .

Above all, we bewail the fact that the great disasters about to befall us barely leave a trace on the intellectual reflection of our time. It's as if we were going to live forever, but the real thinker, we agree, knows, without melodrama, that thought is fragile and already touched by death.

Isn't that what the convalescing Rosenzweig knew as he assembled *The Star of Redemption* in his barracks in Freiburg? It took him seven months, that's all. Seven months, and he was also writing a letter a day to his beloved . . .

Freiburg's a terrible place, we agree at the top of the observation tower on the Schlossberg. It was rebuilt to look exactly like it was before the bombing, that's the problem, W. decides, and compares it unfavourably to Plymouth, which was rebuilt in an entirely different style.

W. reminds me of Abercrombie's Plan for Plymouth, published during the war, which saw the city organised in long boulevards, transected by the avenue that runs from the train station to the Hoe. Modernism at its finest, we agree.

But Freiburg's fake. I remind W. of Warsaw, the central part of which was built in an exact replica of what was there before the bombing —weren't we at our happiest eating out with our guide in the old square? —'That's because it was *obviously* fake', W. says. And then there was the warmth and conviviality of the Poles. —'The Freiburgers are cold, cold!'

Last night, we worked our way through all the wines on the menu, glass by glass. In the end, the Polish waiter sat down with us and told us the bar was terrible. He was keen to try his English: 'My heart, how do you say it? (he makes the gesture, and we say "aches") *aches* for you. Go somewhere else'.

Where should we go? In moments of crisis, W. always asks himself what Kafka would do. What would Kafka do in our place? What would he make of it all? But that's the point: Kafka would never find himself in our place; he would never have made the mistakes we've made.

Kafka was at least a man of Europe, of old Europe. A Europe in crisis, but Europe nonetheless. And us? What does Europe mean to us? What could it ever mean? We're lost in Europe, two apes, two fools, though one is infinitely more foolish than the other.

We have to get away. But where to? W. takes the situation in hand.

Strasbourg soothes us. Strolling through the wide boulevards, we grow calm and quiet. So many beautiful buildings, one after another! It's too much, we're dwarfed, humbled . . . and for a time, we're quiet, really quiet, lost in wonder at old Europe.

The phrase, *old Europe*, is an oxymoron, W. and I decide. The Europeans live in history, as we do not. What can we do but pass across its surface like skaters? Its historical depth is something of which we are only half-aware, we decide. It troubles us, it makes us feel uneasy, but in the end we can have no relationship to it.

What did we say to the European professor who asked a whole circle of us how many languages we spoke, rather than read? We can read a whole bunch of languages . . ., that's what we said. That's not what he asked, he said. Not one of us *spoke* a single language. Most of us hadn't really been to Europe. None of us thought of ourselves as Europeans . . .

He was disgusted, of course, W. says. We were disgusted with ourselves. We were mired in self-disgust, our whole circle. We hung our heads. If we could have hung ourselves at that moment, we would have done so.

Strasbourg. Isn't this where Levinas and Blanchot met for the first time? We remember the photo of them both from Malka's biography: two students, the one tall and thin, the other cheerful and plump; one dishevelled in a double breasted suit and the other dressed like a dandy with a silver-knobbed cane . . .

'Compare our friendship', says W., 'to that of Levinas and Blanchot'. Of their correspondence, only a handful of letters survive. Of ours, which take the form of obscenities and drawings of cocks exchanged on Microsoft Messenger, everything survives, though it shouldn't. Of their near daily exchanges, nothing is known; of our friendship, everything is known, since I, like an idiot, put it all on the internet.

Blanchot was above all discreet, but I am indiscretion itself; Levinas barely spoke of his friend, but I am gossip and idle talk itself. Whereas both men were immensely modest, and weighed everything they said with great consideration, I am immensely *im*modest, and weigh nothing I say or write with any consideration at all. Whereas both wrote with great care and forethought, I write with neither care nor forethought, being seemingly proud of my immense idiocy.

Suddenly, we are weary. Old Europe is immeasurably greater than us, we know that. Who hasn't walked in these streets? What hasn't happened here? European history flows through the city like a great river. And what of us, carried along like two turds in that river?

We sit down in a bistro and drink Alsatian wine from tumblers. W. speaks his bad French softly, and we dream, for a moment, that we are real European intellectuals.

In they come, depressive weather systems from the Atlantic, reaching W. first (in the southwest of England) before reaching me (in the northeast of England), bringing grey days with constant rain. The Westerlies are destroying us, we agree. When will it end?

This summer, W. tells me on the phone, he's become even more stupid than usual. He's reading Cohen in German on the infinitesimal calculus. But he barely understands German! He barely understands maths! The English mathematical terms he finds in his dictionary to translate the German ones are just as opaque. What does it all mean?, W. wonders.

I've been thinking only of administration, I tell him. It's my only concern, I tell him. It's taken me over. It's all to do with my periods of unemployment, W. thinks. It's what I most fear, unemployment. —'You could only have become an administrator', W. says. 'You developed the soul for it. The fear'.

My administrative zeal frightens him, W. admits. It's a sign of complete desperation. In the end, it's what will always compromise my real work, my reading and writing. —'You always have administration to fall back on', W. says. 'You never really experience your failure'.

With neither a fear of unemployment nor a fearful skill as an administrator, W. is alone with his failure, he says. It's terrible—there's no alibi, he can't blame it on anyone. Whose fault is it but his? W. laments his laziness, his indolence. He had every advantage and now—what has he accomplished? What has he done?

I can have no understanding of his sense of failure, W. tells me. None. It's beyond me. —'You're like the dog that licks the hand of its master. You'll be licking their hand even as they beat you, and making little whiny noises. You're good at that, aren't you—making whiny noises?'

He sees me in his mind's eye, W. says. I pause from my ceaseless administrative work, look up for a moment . . . Of what am I thinking?, W. says. What's struck me? But he knows I'm only full of administrative anxieties, and my pause is only a slackening of the same relentless movement.

And what of him, when he looks up from his labours? What does he see? Of what is he dreaming? Of thought, W. says. Of a single thought, from which something might begin. Of a single thought that might justify his existence.

Absurdly grateful—that's the phrase that sums it up, W. says. Take my life, the misery of my life—take what little I've achieved, what little chance I had, and what little I've accomplished despite that lack of opportunity—and still, I'm *absurdly grateful.*

I'm grateful for my flat, for the squalor in which I live. I'm grateful for the damp that streams down the walls and the rats that crawl over one another in my back yard. And with my solitude, my misery, the fact I speak to no one, the fact that no one speaks to me—it's exactly the same: I'm *absurdly grateful.*

'You're surprised even to have got this far', W. says, that's what horrifies him. This far—but how far have I got? If anything, I've gone *backwards;* I've ended up with less than I had before. I've subtracted something from the world. Haven't I taken from W.? Haven't I deprived him of some important part of his own ability?

I'll thank them as they kick me in the teeth, W. says. But I'll thank them, too, when they kick W. in the teeth. A friend of mine deserves nothing else, that's how I think of it, isn't it? Down we fall, further and yet further. Down— another step, and down again—W. didn't know there were any more steps—and thanking them all the way . . .

Of course, I should take my life immediately, that would be the honourable thing, W. says. I should climb the footstool to the noose . . . But it would already be too late, that's the problem, W. says. The sin has already been committed. The sin against existence, against the whole order of existing things.

That I should have lived at all is a disgrace, W. says. It's *the* disgrace, the disgrace of disgraces. But about the fact that I *do* exist, nothing can be done.

He could stab me. In fact he's offered several times. Sometimes I've asked him to. Sometimes I've proposed a double suicide: he stabbing me, and I him. But then, of course, it would do nothing; it's already too late. There's only the fact that I exist, and the fact that his, W.'s, existence has already been *utterly contaminated* by my existence.

A double suicide—is that the answer? But who would stab who first? Who would string up the nooses? And could W. be sure, really sure, that I was really prepared to die as he was? Or even that *he* would be prepared to die as *I* apparently was?

Death seems as far away from us as ever. When will it end?, W. wonders. Isn't the end overdue? Shouldn't it have come already? When the apocalypse comes, it will be a relief, W. says. We'll close our eyes at last. There'll be no more need to apologise, or to account for ourselves. No guilt . . .

It's our fault, it's all our fault, we should at least admit that, W. says. It's our fault and particularly mine. *My* fault, W. says, because my existence couldn't help but contaminate his. And *his* fault, somewhat at least, because he continues to allow his existence to be contaminated by mine.

But what can we do about it? To whom should we apologise? Each other? I should certainly apologise to him, W. says. I owe him a lifetime of apologies. But doesn't he owe me an apology, too? Doesn't he, by his continual presence in my life, *perpetuate the disaster*?

He gives me license, W. says. He gives me encouragement—but why? In the end, perhaps I'm only a figment of his imagination, a kind of nightmare, he says. Can't you see I'm burning?, I ask him in his dream. But in the end, he's burning, W. says. He's the one who set himself on fire.

Every summer, he begins work with great ambition, W. says. He'll read more than ever, and more deeply! He'll write as he's never written before! But by the end of the summer, it's all gone wrong. Why does he never learn?, W. muses. Why does nothing change?

It's a great mystery to him, W. says, his eternal capacity for hope and the eternal destruction of his capacity for hope. He lives and dies a whole lifetime over summer, W. says, and is reborn every autumn, a little more stupid.

How are his studies of messianism progressing?, I ask W. on the phone. He's burrowing back through Rosenzweig and Cohen to Schelling, he says, whose books he can only get hold of in Gothic script. He can barely read Gothic script, he says. It drives him crazy. But nevertheless, he's made some discoveries. —'It's all to do with infinite judgements', he says. 'And the infinitesimal calculus'.

Above all, messianism's got nothing to do with mysticism, says W. He can't abide mysticism. —'It's maths, it's all about maths!' He can't do maths, W. says. This is the great flaw which prevents him really understanding messianism. But then too it might have something to do with the two kinds of negative in ancient Greek, W. says. The two kinds of privation, the second of which is not really a kind of privation. 'It's like the *in-* of infinite', W. says mysteriously, 'which is not simply an *absence* of the finite'.

But W.'s studies of ancient Greek are not progressing well, he says. It's the aorist, it defeats him every time. W.'s bumping his head against the ceiling of his intelligence, he says. I often have that feeling, I tell him. —'No, you're just lazy', W. says.

'What are your thoughts on messianism?', asks W. I don't have any thoughts on messianism, I tell him. What about him? W. isn't able to think about messianism, he says. He's not capable of it, and neither am I.

Perhaps that's all messianism could mean to us: the possibility that one day we might be changed so radically that we would be able to think about messianism, says W.

'What have you done today?', W. asks me. 'How do you actually spend your time?' Weeks and months and years pass, but I seem to do nothing, W. says. 'What have you read? What have you written, and why haven't you sent me any of it?'

'Friends should send each other what they write', W. says. He sends me everything—*everything*, and I barely even read it. He doesn't know why he thanked me in the acknowledgements of his new book, he says. I tell him I was surprised to find myself thanked as part of a long list of friends and colleagues. Didn't I single him out in my acknowledgements for *very special thanks*?

W. says I didn't even read the chapters he sent to me. He could tell: my remarks were too general. I did read them, I tell him, well, nearly all of them. —'You didn't read chapter five', says W., 'with the dog'. He was very proud of his pages on his dog, even though he doesn't own a dog. 'You should always include a dog in your books', says W.

It's a bit like his imaginary children in his previous book, W. says. —'Do you remember the passages on children?' Even W. wept. He weeps now to think of them. He's very moved by his own imaginary examples, he says.

He wants to work a nun into his next book, he says. An imaginary nun, the kindest and most gentle person in the world.

What we lack in intellectual ability and real knowledge, we make up for in pathos, W. says.

He's learnt everything he knows about pathos from me, he says. He can make himself weep at the pathos of his writing. I must be constantly weeping, W. says, night and day, since my writing is based only on pathos and has virtually no other content.

Yes, I am a pathetic thinker, W. says, if I can be called a thinker at all. Of course, so is he. He learned it from me. In its way, it's quite impressive—the way everything I say is marked with urgency, as though it were the last thing I will ever say! As though I were going to expire at any moment!

Then there's the way I raise my voice in my presentations, reaching great bellowing crescendos entirely arbitrarily, W. says. They bear no relation to what I'm actually saying. And then I like to go all quiet, too, don't I?, W. says. All hushed! As if I'd drawn everyone back to the dawn of creation! As if something momentous were about to happen!

All in all, it's always an amazing performance from me, W. says. I always look as though I want to start a cult. *Schwärmerei*, W. says, that's what marks everything I write. It means swarm *and* enthusiasm, W. says. I'm one of the enthusiasts that Kant hated. It's all *Schwärmerei* with me, isn't it?, W. says.

Sometimes he thinks it's because I'm working class. I can't get over the idea someone is actually listening to me, W. says, that I have an audience. Which, come to think of it, *is* rather extraordinary. I think I'm speaking to people better than me, more refined. Which is, of course, almost always true. I hate them and I love them, W. says; I want only their approval, but at the same time I don't want it; it's the last thing I want.

W. has his pathetic moments, he admits. Sometimes he feels the *Schwärmerei* rising in his breast. Sometimes his voice begins to climb the decibels. But then he knows that I am to follow him, and who will notice his excesses then? I make audiences flinch, he says. I make them twitch in involuntary horror. All that *Schwärmerei*! All that pathos!

It's our great fortune to live at the periphery, W. and I agree. He feels an enormous love for his city in the southwest and I feel an enormous love for my city in the northeast. Conversely, I am always overjoyed to visit his city just as he is always overjoyed to visit mine. There's nothing better than visiting a city at the periphery, W. says, just as there's nothing worse than visiting a city at the centre (although, he grants, there are peripheries to every centre).

And there is our own peripheriness, W. and I agree. We are essentially peripheral. Who is threatened by us? Who bothers with us? No one, we agree. We have been completely left alone. No one watches out for us, but on the other hand, no one has really noticed us, so we can get up to whatever we like. We are blips on no one's radar. Our fates matter to no one, and perhaps not even to ourselves. That's one thing that marks us very strongly, we agree: indifference to our own fates.

For haven't we noticed that the world is shit? Isn't it the most obvious thing that it's all going to shit? You can't struggle against it. You can't do anything at all. Those at the centre don't realise it. They haven't grasped their essential powerlessness. Only we have grasped it, we who live at the periphery of our own interests, no longer advancing our own cause.

For what would that be: *our own cause*? What could we want in a world of shit? First of all, distrust yourself, burrow down. Destroy all vestiges of hope, of the desire for salvation. Because it will not come good. It's leading nowhere. Nothing means anything. The centre does not matter. There's suffering everywhere—agreed. There's suffering and horror everywhere—on that we're agreed. But the first step must be to peripherise ourselves, and to peripherise ourselves with respect to ourselves.

W.'s street. The houses at the bottom are no longer derelict, he says. You used to be able to see the faces of children behind the cracked windows, like ghosts, but now developers have moved in.

This part of the city was once very wealthy, he says. His house was once owned by a ship's captain, he says—imagine it! We stand back and admire its storeys.

The railway to London used to run through here, he tells me a little later. Passengers would disembark from their cruise liners onto the train, and go straight up to London. The houses are still grand, W. says, although most of them have been turned into flats now. They're full of alcoholics and drug addicts, he says. No one wants to live round here.

Children bang on the window as we sit inside and drink. —'Ignore them', says W., 'don't pay them any attention'. He's not frightened of them, he says later as he closes the shutters. —'They're lost', he says, 'you can see it in their eyes'.

Their grandparents would have moved down from Scotland, like everyone around here, W. explains. Thousands of them came down to the dockyards a couple of generations ago, but there's no work for them now, nothing. So what do they do but drink all day?

He'd drink all day, says W., if he had nothing to do. Sometimes they punch him or throw ashtrays at Sal, but that's alright. He'd be exactly the same, says W.

Sand beneath an exposed cobblestone. Under the paving stones, the beach, I say to W., who's showing me old Plymouth. Not much of the old city survives, W. comments. We pass through a walled medieval garden, with a low maze and a fountain. Alcoholics drink beneath a portico, listening to a radio. There's no one to move them on, W. says. He approves of that.

These are the end times, we both agree. It's enough to be left alone like the alcoholics, but our time will come just as their time will come. We'll be rounded up and shot, W. says.

It's only a matter of time, we know, before we are found out. They haven't really noticed us yet, that's what saves us. But when they do . . . !

The clock is ticking, we agree. —'This is not our time', W. says as we walk through the newly converted Victualling Yard. Who lives in these flats?, we wonder as we pass through the wide boulevards. Who can afford them?

What are the signs of the End?, I ask W. —'You. You are a sign of the End', says W. 'Actually, we both are. The fact that we have careers or flourish at all is a sign of the End. Of course, the fact that we won't have them for much longer is a sign that the End is coming closer'.

There's something sick about us, W. says, something depraved. Only it's not just about us, says W., but about the whole world. We're seismographic, W. says. We register the great horrors of the world in our guts. That's why I'm always about to soil myself, W. says. It's why I have a continual nosebleed and always feel ill.

Many illnesses have coursed through W.'s body. Colds, of course. Myriad flus. Pneumonia, once. Gastroenteritis, twice. We're weak, he says, we're the runts of the litter. Something has come to an end with us. We're the end of the line in some important way.

It all finishes here, W. says, pointing at his body and then pointing at mine. Especially here, says W., pointing his finger at my belly.

My obesity always impresses him, W. says. My greed. The way I eat, the amount I eat. He'd call me a *carnal* man, W. says, but that sounds too grand. —'You're just full of greed'. He wonders what would I be like if I didn't go to the gym?, It's all channelled into my enormous thighs, W. says. They're grotesque. —'You're out of proportion!' And my great fat arms, W. says.

For his part, W. takes no exercise. He hasn't felt well for many years—eleven or twelve, he's not sure how many. There was a time when he'd go for great walks on the moor, he remembers. He had a walking friend, of course. You can't go walking on your own, that would just lead to *enormous melancholy*, he says. In fact, that's what I always say, isn't it: that going out walking on my own would lead to *enormous melancholy*?

W. is no stranger to melancholy, he says. He's essentially agoraphobic. He's only *really* happy holed up in his room, working. He'd prefer never to leave his house, says W. Or indeed his study. He'd like to become a recluse like Howard Hughes, he says, with jars of toenails and bottles of urine. It's only the love of a good woman which saves him from that.

Now and again, he thinks he should walk to work, or cycle. But it's too far, and all uphill. It would only depress him, W. says. In the end, he's not cut out for exercise. He'll lead a short life, says W., as will I. A short, unfulfilled life, which will come to nothing. —'What's it all been for?', W. asks. 'Nothing!', he says. 'Not a thing!'

How much time do we have left? —'Not long', W. says.

'We're not the sort who live long lives. Look at us!' He hasn't felt himself for twenty years, says W., and I've long since run to a fat and bleary-eyed alcoholism. But I am more of a whiner than he is, W. says. There's always something wrong with me, isn't there? One day it's a nosebleed, the next nausea, the next some indeterminate fever . . . And my stomach, whatever is wrong with my stomach?

W. never used to believe me about my stomach. He thought I was a hypochondriac. But once he saw my face turn green—green!—he understood. You looked appalling, he said. Everyone was horrified, everyone at the table. And then, for a terrible morning when he was visiting me, W. himself was taken ill. —'It's my stomach! My God!', he cried. He decided it was my lifestyle. All that drinking! All that eating! One night, he saw me pass out from gluttony. I ate like a maniac, he said, plate after plate. And then my head fell back . . . he was worried, but then he heard me snoring.

'How can you live like this?', said W. exasperated beyond belief. 'How?' I've always maintained that this is my *five year hole*. Everyone should be allowed one of those. Deleuze had one, didn't he? A *five year hole*, that's what he called it, in which he wrote nothing? —'But Deleuze was *working*', says W., 'and you don't do any work, do you? What happened to you? How did you get like this? Why don't you read anymore? Why don't you write?'

W. finds the collapse of his protégé quite fascinating. —'When did it all start going wrong? When did you first become aware of it?' There's something spectacular about my decline, W.

decides. Something Faustian. —'What kind of bargain did you make with the devil back then? How did you appear so intelligent?' And then: 'Well, he's carried your soul off now, hasn't he?'

Then, in a spirit of diagnosis: 'Describe your work day to me. What do you do?' I tell him I get up very early. —'How early?' Never later than six thirty, I tell him. —'I get up at five!', W. says, 'Earlier sometimes!' —Then I do two hours of work, I tell him. —'What kind of work? What does it involve?' I read . . . —'What kind of reading? In the original language? Primary, rather than secondary?' I write . . . —'Ah, that's your problem. You try to write too soon. You have to slow down. Read more slowly. That's why I read things in the original'. Then I go to the office to do my administering, I tell W. —'Ah, your administration', says W., 'that's what stops you from writing your magnum opus, isn't it?'

A little later, in the taxi home: 'Your decline. Where were we? What are your plans? What are you writing?' Nothing, I tell him. I have no plans. —'You should do a book', says W., 'if only so I can hear you whine. I like it when you whine in your presentations. Like a stuck pig, crying out! No, it's more plaintive than that. Like a sad ape. A sad ape locked up with his faeces'.

'Right, you're my eyes', says W., leaving his glasses behind as we set out on our walk. —'All set?' We're all set. Despite his general inactivity, W. is a great advocate of walking: it's what we're made for, he says, and speaks of the long walks he used to take on the weekend.

We're essentially joyful, reflects W. in the ferry to Mount Edgcumbe, that's what saves us. We know we're failures, we know we'll never achieve anything, but we're still joyful. That's the miracle. But why is that?, we muse. Why are we content?'— 'Stupidity', says W. And then: 'We're not ambitious. Are you ambitious?' No, I tell him. —'Well neither am I'.

We head up into the grounds, the great sweep of lawn running up to the mansion on our right, opening up a great landscape, planned and planted two hundred years ago. —'They must have thought they had all the time in the world', says

W. Then, on our left, a beach of pebbles, the sea, and, across the Sound, the distant city, with blue-grey naval ships going to and fro.

'See, what more do you want than this?', says W. Later, rising up into the woods, we sit and look out over the water. There's a ferry, travelling out to Spain. W.: 'We should go on a trip, one day. We should go to Spain'. And then: 'We're not going to go anywhere, are we? We're men of habit. Simple beings'. And then, 'Everything's got to be the same. That's our strength'.

The last Duke of Edgcumbe, W. tells me, married a barmaid from the pub, and put the whole estate up for sale. The city bought it. It's a miracle, we agree, as we walk out along the shore to where the path rises up through the woods.

It was here the Dukes and their guests would drive about in their carriages in the twilight, imagining they were in some Gothic romance. There's even a faux-ruined folly built on the hill, looking very unconvincing in the autumn sun.

A landslide has taken the woods with it; some trees still stand, growing aslant, though most have fallen. The path has been diverted, but W. prefers the old route. It's slow going—very overgrown—and where the cliff has completely collapsed, we have to scramble across scree.

What would happen if we fell? It's a long way down. But W. and I never think about our deaths or anything like that. That would be pure melodrama. Besides, if we died, others would come along to replace us. Our position is structural, we've always been convinced of that. We're only signs or syndromes of some great collapse, and our deaths will be no more significant than those of summer flies in empty rooms.

As we look out to sea, a great shadow seems to move under the water. He can see it, says W.—'Look: the kraken of your idiocy'. Yes, there it is, moving darkly beneath the water.

W. is growing his hair, he says. —'It's what the kids are doing'. The kids are looking very gentle, we agree. It's the age of Aquarius. —'So why aren't you growing yours? Go on, grow it!' This as we mount the Hoe from the town side.

'The sea makes me happy', W. says, 'does it make you happy?' It does. We stand before the whole panorama, from Mount Batten to Mount Edgcumbe, the far off seabreak with the lighthouse at one end, and, because it's a very clear day, the farther lighthouse that can be seen standing blue ten miles out against the horizon. And then the various islands, large and small. And the whole sweep of water, shimmeringly blue under the very blue sky: here we are again!

To think it will all end so soon! To think we're on the edge of the greatest catastrophe! The oceans will boil, the sky will burn away into space. And won't we be the first to be swept away? Won't we be the first to go under?

The apocalypse is close, we know that. The apocalypse is coming, of that we are certain . . .

As we walk towards the lido, W. tells me about the Greek

phalanx. The soldiers locked their shields together, he says, to form a great defensive wall. Their bronze-tipped spears would poke out of the front. Together, loyal, they were almost invincible, says W. —'Of course you wouldn't understand any of this', he says. 'You're not loyal. You know nothing of loyalty. You would break the phalanx', says W. 'You'd be the first to break it'.

W.'s great fantasy, and he must admit, he says, that it *is* a fantasy, is of forming a community of writers and thinkers, linked by mutual friendship. Together we'll be capable of more than we might do on our own. That's what he's always hoped, says W. It's what he's always dreamt of.

Above all, we have to avoid the traps of careerism, says W. Loyalty and trust, that's what matters: we have to be prepared to die for one another. —'Literally that: *to die for one another*', W. says. 'It's all about the phalanx', W. says. 'The phalanx you would immediately betray'.

That's the ultimate paradox, W. observes: that one with such faith in friendship should end up with such a friend. Would I die for him? No. Would I immediately betray him, given any opportunity? Yes. In fact, I've already done so several times.

Where did it all go wrong? At what stage did he stray from the path? These are the questions he asks himself constantly, W. says, and they always come back to the same answer: me. It's my fault, W. says. Everything went wrong when he met me.

'When did you know you were a failure?', W. repeatedly asks

me. 'When was it you knew you'd never have a single thought of your own—not one'?

He asks me these questions, W. says, because he's constantly posing them to himself. Why is he still so amazed at his lack of ability? He's not sure. But he is amazed, and he will never get over it, and this will have been his life, this amazement and his inability to get over it.

What amazes him still further, says W., is that I am almost entirely lacking in the same amazement. I'm like the idiot double of an idiot, W. says, being of the same intelligence (or nearly the same intelligence; I am a few IQ points behind him), of the same degree of laziness (or nearly the same laziness; I am more indolent than he is), but entirely lacking an awareness of what I so signally lack.

Every year I tell W. about my latest plans to escape. It amuses W., who knows I will never escape and nor will he. Why do I think I can escape? Why do I have that temerity? 'You're not getting out', he says, 'you're stuck like everybody else'. Two years ago I was going to learn Sanskrit, he reminds me. I was going to become a *great scholar of Hinduism*. And what was it last year? It was music, wasn't it? I was going to become a *great scholar of music*.

But what did I know about Sanskrit, really? And what did I know about music? —'Nothing at all', says W., 'about either subject'. What work did I do to learn something about Sanskrit and music? —'None at all!', says W. 'Not one bit!'

There's no getting out: when am I going to understand that? I'm stuck forever: when am I going to resign myself to the cage of my stupidity?

W. has been lost in bureaucracy, he says on the phone. He tells me about his recent illness, the most ill he's ever been. —'I don't know how Kafka wrote when he was ill', says W. When W. was ill, he was farther from writing *The Trial* than he's ever been, he says.

In W.'s mind, he says, ill health has always been linked to genius. Maybe it's the key to great thoughts, he says, reminding me of the authors we admire who passed close to death. But then, of course, W. has only got a cold, not even flu, not really, let alone tuberculosis or liver failure or anything like that.

Still, he's disappointed that not one thought has come to him, not one, especially as it would pertain to the great crises that have gripped the world. He always thinks one might. It worked for Kafka, didn't it? And what about Blanchot? But W.'s illnesses lead nowhere, he says. They always disappoint him.

We're off on another trip. —'How many shirts are you taking?', asks W. on the phone. Four, I tell him. Four! He says he'll only take two. He doesn't sweat as much as me, he says. —'You sweat a lot, don't you, fat boy? How many pairs of pants are you taking?' Four, I tell him. —'Four pairs of pants', W. muses. He'll take four as well, he decides, and four pairs of socks. —'How many pairs of trousers will you take?', asks W. One, I tell him. —'One!', W. says, 'after all your accidents? Have you learnt nothing?' W.'s going to take two pairs of trousers, he says, just in case.

On the train to Dundee. 'What are you doing?', says W. I'm playing *Doom* on my mobile phone. —'I haven't seen you open a book for days', W. says. Later, I take some gossip magazines out of my bag. —'Why do you read them?', says W. 'Didn't you bring a book?' W.'s reading *The Star of Redemption* again. —'A proper book!', he says. 'I don't understand it, though'. He shows me unmarked pages. Pages without any annotations, he says, except for question marks, meaning he doesn't understand, and exclamation marks, meaning he's totally lost.

'So what are you reading, then? Who's that?' Jordan, the model, I tell him. —'Who's that?' Peter André. —'Oh yes, I like them, they're funny'. He laughs at the pictures of grossly obese women on the next page. 'That's you in a few years', he says. 'When do you think you're going to get as fat as that? It's going to happen, isn't it, the way you're going?'

'You need a man bag', says W., and shows me his. 'You see? You can fit everything into it. Everything and anything'. His bag sits on his hip, and hangs from a leather strap round his shoulders. He decides we should spend the day before the conference looking for a man bag for me. —'You need to smarten up'. Rucksacks won't do. Man bags are the thing. —'And you should get rid of that jacket'.

'So, what have you got in your rucksack?', W. asks. 'Go on, show me, I could do with a laugh'. I take out another gossip magazine, and then another. He gasps in horror. —'My God, there's no hope for you'.

Then some snacks. Nuts, first of all. —'What kind of nuts are those? Can I have some?' Then popcorn. —'Popcorn? No wonder you're getting fat'. Then pretzels. —'Where do you think you're going? Up Everest?' Then a book. —'Load of shit! You read too much secondary stuff'. Then my notebook. W. is very pleased with this. —'Let's have a look'.

He flips through the pages. Drawings of cocks, of monkey butlers. He'd taken it from me at a presentation in order to formulate his Hebrew question before he asked it. —'Ah, my Hebrew question! My finest hour!' He'd quoted from the book of Genesis from memory, in Hebrew, like a real scholar, we both remember that. Something about the *tohu vavohu*, wasn't that it? —'The *tohu vavohu*', says W., 'exactly'.

Then he tosses the notebook aside. —'So, what thoughts have you had? Tell me. I need entertaining'.

We read the papers. Our stomachs hurt. A few days in my company, says W., and he feels iller than he's ever felt. —'Drunk and then ill. Drunk and then ill . . . That's your life, isn't it? How do you do it? How can you live like this?'

What has he got in his man bag?, I ask W. —'I'll show you'. He places a large notebook on the desk. In the front, he says, he writes the ideas of others in black ink, and in the back, in red ink, he develops his own ideas.

How many ideas has he had? He opens the notebook for me. —'Mmm. Quite a few'. —'Can I copy some out?' W. says I can. *A book must produce more thought than it itself has*, I write. *The messianic is the conjunction of time and politics*, I write. And the best one, *It might be better to speak of a negative eschatology. Anticipation of the future as disaster*—I copy that out, too.

Are those ideas?, I ask him. They're on the way to ideas, W. says. W. asks to see my notes. —'What's this drawing of a cock supposed to mean?'

Next, W. takes out *The Star of Redemption*. —'I don't understand a word. Not—a—word. I don't suppose you can help me, either'. Next, he sets down a packet of moisturising wipes. What else? —'Nothing else. But I've got room for everything in my man bag'. I tell W. his man bag is very continental. —'Oh yes, I'll bet Rosenzweig had one. And Kafka'.

Before beginning to give our collaborative presentations, W. and I always dab our wrists and then the skin behind our ears with moisturising wipes. It calms you down, W. says. It prepares you for the task ahead. He takes his wipes everywhere with him. —'I learned it from Sal. You see—this is what women can teach you'.

They were handy when we were travelling across Poland. We sat there with flushed faces until W. got his tissues out. —'Dab your wrists, where women put on perfume, and then behind your ears', W. told us, giving out tissues. Suddenly a marvellous coolness descended. —'You see!'

'Why don't you get rid of that jacket?', says W. 'You've been wearing it for years. It makes you look fat. It's completely shapeless'.

W. and I are wearing our flowery shirts. 'Look at us', W. sighs, 'fat and blousy, and everyone else slim and wearing black'.

What's wrong with us? Why are we never dressed for thought? Take my trousers, for example. They should be pulled up round my waist like those of Benjamin in that famous photograph. But they sag. They droop disappointingly. —'You're a man without hips!', says W. 'A man without ideas!'

I'm getting fat, of course. Eventually, I'll have to wear elasticated trousers like the American professors, W. says. Perhaps it will suit me, my obesity. Perhaps it will give me gravitas.

It's too hot!, I complain. W. reaches in his man bag for a wipe. W.'s prepared for the heat, he says. He watched the weather forecasts. 'Dundee is either very hot', he says, 'or very cold'. He reaches in his man bag for suntan lotion, and applies it to his cheerful face.

W. is an enemy of sunglasses. —'Take them off', he says, 'you look like an idiot'. But it's sunny, I protest. —'They block your pineal eye', he says. 'It needs sunlight'.

The pineal eye's in the centre of the head, W. explains, but it's sensitive to light. Without light, you quickly become depressed. —'That's why you're so morose', says W. I'm morose, he says, whereas he, who doesn't wear sunglasses, is joyful. —'Joy is everything', W. says. He is essentially joyful.

'I'll bet it smells terrible out there', says W., looking out of the window of my flat. 'It does, doesn't it? You can tell. I'll bet it really stinks'. You'd never know of course from inside the flat, he says, because the windows won't open. They're jammed shut, I tell him, by the flat changing shape. It's sinking, I tell him. It's collapsing in the middle.

Later, W. helps me empty the cupboards in preparation for the damp proofers. We have to strip the flat down to a bare frame, I tell him. —'God, what's that smell?', asks W. as he sets down the pots and pans I pass him in the other room. 'These are filthy', he says. 'How could you let them get like this?'

W.'s worried about my cough. —'The damp's turning you consumptive', he says. Even *he's* developing a cough, and he's only been here a few hours. —'How can you live like this? How can you get anything done?'

W.'s house is perfectly made for work, he says. His quiet,

book-lined study on the second floor; his desk and laptop; the view over Plymouth roofs is perfect inspiration, he says. He has a sense of living above the world rather than living below it in the mud, as I do.

'All your worldly possessions', says W., looking round the room. 'Is this what you've amounted to?' Pots and pans, sticky with filth; rusty tins of mackerel and tomatoes; a duvet soaked in spilt fabric conditioner: 'Yes, this is what it's come to', W. says, 'it all ends here'.

I must have a death-drive, W. surmises. That's the only thing that could explain it. I must, on some level, want to destroy myself. —'Just throw this stuff out', W. says, 'all of it. You don't cook here, do you?' There's no power in the kitchen, I tell him. There's no electricity. —'My God. How can you live like this?', says W., his voice high with incredulity. 'It wouldn't have got this bad if you lived with someone'.

It's no wonder I don't do any work, W. says. He couldn't work if he lived like me. Out all the time, reading nothing and living in squalor. It really is disgusting, he says. And the damp! He's never seen anything like it, W. says. It hits you as soon as you come in. No wonder I'm always ill.

'What would Béla Tarr would think of your damp?', W. says. 'What would he make of it?' W. has become obsessed with Béla Tarr. He's a genius, says W. He says he only makes films about poor, ugly people. The ugly and poor are *his* people, that's what he says, says W.

Béla Tarr was going to be a philosopher. But when he started making films . . . No abstraction for him, says W.

He's completely devoted to the concrete, says W. To what he sees in front of him. He's not like us, W. says. He doesn't float nebulously into the most general and most confused of ideas, into our *clouds of unknowing*.

'Béla Tarr doesn't believe in God', says W. 'He's seen too much to believe in God'. A little later, 'He takes years over each film', says W. 'Years! Every kind of obstacle is placed in his way. His producers die of despair. His cinematographers leave in disgust. He runs out of money'. And then, 'His films are full of drunks. Full of drunk, aggressive people like you', says W. 'And mud. His films are full of mud. That's where you belong', says W., 'in the mud'.

Béla Tarr made his first film when he was sixteen, W. says. Sixteen! Sixteen! That's when he started, says W. —'When did you know', says W., 'when did you know you'd never amount to anything?' When did I take refuge in vague and cloudy ideas that have nothing to do with the world?

There's something *absolute* about my yard, W. says. You can't get beyond it. Some great process has completed itself there. —'What did you do to those plants? Desecrate them?' and then, 'What's hung over your washing line? What was it, before it started rotting?', and then, 'Were those once bin bags? My God, what have they become?'

Béla Tarr would discern what is absolute about my yard, W. says. He'd register its every detail in a twenty minute tracking shot. The sewage, the concrete, the bin bags and rotting plants . . . the yard would mean more to Béla Tarr than all our nonsense.

Béla Tarr said that the walls, the rain and the dogs in his films have their own stories, which are much more important than so-called human stories. He said that the scenery, the weather, the locations and time itself *have their own faces*. Their own faces! Yes, we're agreed, the yard, the horror of the yard, is the only thing around here in which Béla Tarr would be interested.

W. sends me a quotation to *mull over in my stupidity*, he says.

Forms of behaviour such as opportunism and cynicism derive from this infinite process in which the world becomes no more than a supermarket of opportunities empty of all inherent value, yet marked by the fear that any false move may set in motion a vortex of impotence.

W. finds the phrase, *vortex of impotence*, particularly thought-provoking, he says. It describes my entire life: action and powerlessness, movement and paralysis; that strange combination of despair and frenzy.

I want to escape, that's my primary impulse, W. observes. I know something's wrong, fundamentally wrong, and I want to be elsewhere. Of course, he's not like me, says W., the rat who leaves the sinking ship. But I'm not escaping, says W. I'm going to drown with everyone else, he'll make sure of it. I'm going *down*, says W.

We're at the Mill on the Exe, right on the river, the sun shining warmly on our faces.

The South West! W. exclaims. He feels fortunate to live here. The South West is the *graveyard of ambition*, a colleague warned him upon his arrival from the east, but W. is not ambitious.

He just wants a little time and space to work, to think. To try to think, W. says. He reads in his study for three hours a day, he says, and he's content with that. And occasionally he writes a thought in his notebook, at the back, in red ink.

'What about you?', W. asks. 'Where do you write your thoughts?' I tell him I'm too troubled to think. W. says he's troubled too, who isn't? But neither of us really is troubled, W. says. He always thinks of us as joyful, he says.

Drunk in the sun, we offer encomiums to one another. I never make him feel anything other than joyful, says W. I tell him he is able to momentarily make me forget my troubles and that this is his great gift.

W. and I are celebrants of rivers, and always feel the need to hail them. —'The mighty Tyne!', W. might say, and I might say, 'the mighty Plym!' The sight of a river is always an occasion. So, of course, is that of the sea. It's the ozone, says W., it makes you feel alive.

It does, and in particular the view of the sheet of the sea, just past Exeter. The whole sheet of the sea, viewed from the train, neat Plymouth Gin and ice in our plastic cups. —'This is happiness', says W. Of course, they'll have to reroute the trains soon. They're electrical and short circuit when the surf splashes over them. Sometimes they stop for hours, immobile on the track. —'It's the new trains', says W. 'They're shit'.

W.'s felt ill nearly all his adult life, he says. When was the last time he felt well?, I ask him. He can't remember. —'It's been years', he says suddenly. 'Years!' He used to go for great walks on the moors, he remembers. That's when he last felt healthy: on his great weekend walks, when he would set off with his walking friend (whatever happened to him?) with no particular end in view. They'd just walk for miles across the moors.

There's nothing better, he says, than to climb up to the moors, and see the blue strip of the sea in the distance. Are there really big cats up there, panthers and the like? He never saw any, he says. There might be. But his moor walks are long since over. He lacks something, W. says. There's something missing in him. Why doesn't he go on his great moor walks any more?, he wonders, as we look out to sea.

It's important to hail rivers, we both agree, but just as important to hail the sea, although we do not do so by name. We do not, for instance, hail the sea south of Edinburgh as the North Sea, or the sea south of Exeter as the Atlantic (is it the Atlantic?, I ask W. It is, he says.). A simple, 'The sea!' is enough. Just as when we see the edge of the moor on our train journeys in Devon, we cry, 'The moor!'

Ah, the moor! W. is feeling regretful again. How can he become a better person, a better friend? How might he become a better thinker? His life is full of regret, he says, and gets out his Cohen. He's going to read now, he tells me, and I'll have to entertain myself.

On the train, W. and I sip Plymouth Gin from plastic cups. —'How come you got more ice than me?' He reaches over and grabs a handful of mine.

Meanwhile, his book lies unread on the table. —'Cohen', sighs W., 'that's what I should be reading, instead of talking idiocies with you'.

Then he tells me about calculus and God. —'Calculus: that's why Cohen thought God existed. It's all about maths!' W.'s dad tried to teach him calculus, but he didn't understand a word. —'I wasn't ready'. W.'s found an instructional website now. He does exercises.

A little later he says, 'We're not religious. We've got no interest in religion. We're not capable of religious belief'.

We know what genius is, says W. aphoristically, but we know we're not geniuses. It's a gift, he says, but it's also a curse. We can recognise genius in others, but we don't have it ourselves.

Max Brod, so unselfish in his promotion of Kafka, yet so given to a vague and general pathos—to amorphous stirrings wholly alien to the precision of the writing of his friend—has always served as both our warning and our example.

What could he understand of Kafka? Weren't his interpretative books—which did so much to popularise the work of his friend—at every turn, a betrayal of Kafka? But then again, didn't Kafka depend upon his friendship and his support? Didn't Kafka lean on his friend in times of despair and solitude?

We too, W. and I decided long ago, must give our lives in the service of others. We too must write interpretative essays on the work of others more intelligent and gifted than we will ever be. We too must do our best to offer support and solace to others despite the fact that we will always misunderstand their genius, and only bother them with our enthusiasm.

W. finds me in a despondent state on the phone. Yet another of my escape bids has been thwarted. Yet another dream completely dashed. My lines of flight always go splat! against the wall, don't they?, W. observes. I'm like the cartoon mouse who hits the wall and then slides down it, he says. It's painful to see, but also funny.

'That look on your face!', says W. And then: 'Everyone can see it coming, even you can see it coming, but you run up against the same wall, don't you? Every time! The same wall!'

We're bottom feeders, W. always insists. We survive on scraps others leave us. That we can survive from day to day is miracle enough, W. says, let alone have any dreams of escape. We're not even opportunists, he says, we're too stupid for that.

We like to pretend we have some control over the circumstances of our lives, W. says, whereas in reality we have
no control whatsoever. W. understands all this very well, he
says. He learned it from me, which is why he's surprised by
my lapse.

We all have to face it at some time or another, W.
says, there's nowhere for us to go. No up and no down.
We don't have a chance. As soon as I realise this, W. says,
something may be possible. But then again, nothing may be
possible after all.

W. has wheedled £2,600 from some academic fund or other.
It's time to *give* something to the world, he says, rather than
taking. Because that's what we always do, he says, we *take*
from the world.

We should send the money to Béla Tarr! Send it all to
him! Béla Tarr's our leader. How long have we been waiting for a leader? But there he is, working in Hungary, on the
central plain, a long way from us. No doubt his producers
have deserted him. No doubt he's lost another cinematogra-
pher . . . We're agreed: he needs our support, and we need
his leadership.

But how are we going to get the money to Béla Tarr?
Should we go to Hungary ourselves? My God, says W., what
would he make of us? Two buffoons on the central plain!
What would he think? Isn't life hard enough for him as it is?

He uses non-professional actors, says W. of Béla Tarr. We
talk of the great speech in *Damnation* about coal scuttles and
suicide. It's the best scene I've ever seen in a film, I tell him.

He agrees. And the bit in the mud with the dog, with Karrer on all fours barking at the dog. Nothing better. Because that's where we'll end up—in the mud, covered in mud, barking! At each other, if no one else! Barking—in the mud!

W. says he was so alone over Christmas he forgot how to talk. —'I'm not like you', he says, 'I don't *need people*'.

He's written about Spinoza, says W. What have I written about? He sends me his lecture notes. He sends me a paper by someone cleverer than us. He sends me his introduction to a special edition of a journal. That's what he's been doing. He's been busy. Not like me. —'I'll tell you what your problem is', says W., 'you're lazy! Lazy!'

Then W. tests me on Spinoza: What is a mode? What's a substance? What's an attribute? I tell him the *Ethics* is too hard. Get the *Routledge Guidebook to Spinoza's Ethics*, W. tells me. —'But that'll be too hard for you, won't it? Get the *Idiot's Guide to Spinoza*, then. But that'll be too hard, too. Start with these letters on a piece of paper: *S-P-I-N-O-Z-A*. Ponder that in your stupidity'.

'How's your damp?', W. asks. 'Tell me about your flat again. It's shit, isn't it? You've got the worst flat of anyone I've ever met. My God, I don't know how you live there. What's causing it? Do you have any idea?'

It's a mystery, I tell W. I called six damp proofing companies in turn, I tell him, one after another. The water's getting in behind the rendering, said one. You'll have to strip it off, repoint the brick, and render it again. It's the holes in your wall, said another, referring to the long scar left where the lead pipe had to be pulled away.

It's your hopper, said yet another, showing me a thick patch of green on the top of the pipe through which it drained. Ah yes, I said, I tell W., impressed at his observational powers. Do nothing, said another; let the wall breathe. But *I* need to breathe!, I tell W. *I* need to take a single non-damp breath! I've got spores in my lungs! They're coated in mildew!

A *fifth* pressed his nose to the brown plaster in the bathroom. He put his hand on its wet surface. He sniffed. It's condensation that's causing it, he said. Condensation, I said, behind all this? The flat all around us, brown-walled with damp. People underestimate condensation, said the damp whisperer. In a flat like this, with the double-glazing, there's nowhere for water to escape.

He told me about the dew point, I tell W. He told me how the wall comes forward to offer itself to the touch of condensation. I imagined a runner breasting the finish line, I tell W. I imagined a swordfish leaping from the sea.

But the *sixth* interpreter said he thought it was *penetrating* damp, the sort that permeates through pasty brick and the gaps between bricks. Penetrating, coming through, a brown, persistent wave . . .

Damp calls for a Talmudic inquiry; I go from one wise man to another, from one to another, but none is really certain of the Law.

One of us is dragging the other down, W. and I decide, but which one? Is it him or me? His friends say that since he's been hanging out with me, his work's really gone downhill. People are avoiding us, says W. They can smell failure.

I'm going to be found out, that's what I worry about, says W. Someone's going to find out about me and shoot me, W. says, it's only right. '*How have I survived this long?*', W. says, 'that's your only thought. *By what miracle have I survived?*'

W. has thought up many excuses for me. He's had to account for me at length to his friends. Explain him!, they demand. What's going on? And W. has to explain, as best he can, how it all started, how our collaboration began.

But what can he say, really? There's a limit to every

explanation, which is to say the sheer physical fact of my existence. —'There you are', says W. And before that fact, what can anyone do but shrug?

'Thought should bear upon what matters most', says W. as we look out to sea. 'What matters most to you?', asks W. 'Your dinner? Alcohol? Chav mags?'

What matters most, W. muses, are the coming End Times. The ecological disaster and the financial disaster. —'They're nearly upon us', he says. 'Are you ready for the End Times?' Is he? Least of all him, W. says. Least of all us.

We'll be the first to go under, W. says. The very first. He'll welcome it, says W., as judgement for our miserable lives and the immensity of our failure.

'You're never witty', says W., 'that's a sign of intelligence: wit'. W. says he is sometimes witty, but, more generally, he's never witty. I never bring it out in him, W. says. I don't make him more intelligent.

W. is more intelligent than me, he decides. But what about those illuminated moments when the clouds part, and I have ideas? It's true, I do have moments of illumination, W. grants, but they are sporadic and lead nowhere.

Sometimes, W. concedes, it's *as if* I have ideas. I once spoke to him very movingly about the *Phaedrus*, for example, and the reason why Socrates had to leave the city to talk to his friend.

W. immediately lays claim in his essays to any idea I might have. I would do the same, he says. But of course, my ideas are always wrong. They're full of pathos, he says, and they sound correct, but in fact they are no such thing. —'You always get the Greek wrong. Always'.

But sometimes, for a moment, the clouds do clear. —'You manage to speak sense', says W., 'or something like sense'.

'There was that time in the pub in Oxford', W. remembers. 'We all fell silent and listened in wonder. Not to *what* you said, which may or may not have been sensible, and in fact probably wasn't—it was probably the usual pathos and hot air—but *that* you could say it'.

'You of all people. No one expects it of you. Quite the opposite in fact. Which is why it's so surprising'. W. himself was amazed. And there was that time on the long pier at Mount Batten. —'The clouds parted. You spoke sense for nearly an hour'. What did I speak about? W. can't remember. But he'd been amazed, he remembered that.

'Write it down!, write it down!' W. often cries during my moments of illumination, but when I read back my notes, I find only incomprehensible scrawls and random words without sense.

When I die, W. says, he's going to be my literary executor. Delete, delete, delete, that's what he's going to do.

Which one of us is Kafka and which Brod?, W. muses. We're both Brod, he says, and that's the pity of it. Brods without Kafka, and what's a Brod without a Kafka?

We are both Brod, W. says, and Brod for one another. When an ass looks into the gospels, no apostle looks back; when Brod looks into Kafka, it's only Brod who looks back. I am his Brod, W. tells me, but he is my Brod, too.

I am his idiot, but he is mine, and it's this we share in our joy and laughter, as we wake each day into the morning of our idiocy, wiping the sleep from our eyes and stretching.

'These are the last days', says W. 'It's all finished. Everything's so shit', says W., 'but we're happy—why is that? Because we're puerile', he says. 'Because we're inane. It saves us', W. says, 'but it also condemns us'.

We've been singled out for something, W. has decided. We've been marked. Look at us in our flowery shirts, and everyone else slim and wearing black.

We're men of the end, W. says. Do we take nothing seriously? Not even ourselves. Least of all that, says W.

W. reminds me of when I inspected his teaching. He drew diagrams for the students, two stick men. What was he explaining? Hegel and religion, he thinks. —'This is Lars', he said, and drew a tiny cock on one of the stick men, 'and this is me', he said, and drew a huge cock on the other.

'Why do you think we're so puerile?', he asks me later. We've always cursed our sense of humour. We're not witty, we know that. It lets us down. We disappoint everyone.

W.'s got a higher IQ than me, he's decided. A few points higher: that makes all the difference, he says. Intellectually, he stands slightly higher than I do; he has a wider view, a greater panorama. But perhaps this is why he despairs more than I do, and has a keener sense of his failure.

He can see more, says W., and he can also see himself in the context of the whole. He can see the great achievements of the past heaving up behind him like a plateau, and the open space from which great achievements will come in the future. And he can see his own inability to contribute in any way to these achievements, and that, indeed, he is a living obstacle in his body and soul to anything that might happen.

If W.'s on his dung heap perched up and looking around like a meerkat, he says, I'm still playing in the dung. What could I understand of achievement or failure or any of these issues?, W. says. What can I understand of the *magnitude* of our failure?

'What do you think your effect is on others?', W. asks. 'Do you motivate them, inspire them, spur them on? Do you make them think more than they could think on their own? Does the fact of your friendship change the way in which they see the world or vice versa?'

Every time he meets someone (except me), W. asks himself how he could have been kinder, better and more gracious. Every time he thinks of his friends (except me), he asks himself what he might do to help them or to look after them better; he asks himself what he might do to further their thought or their writing.

'What does friendship mean to you, really?', W. asks. 'Do you think you're capable of it? Do you think you've ever been a friend to anyone? Can you even conceive of what being a friend might mean?': these questions constantly pass through his head, W. says, as he knows they do not pass through mine.

Friendship makes the highest demands upon him, says W. It's a kind of test. It's the only chance for him, friendship, says W.; that and love. Love and friendship are the only things that might redeem him, W. says. —'And what about you?', he says. 'How will you redeem yourself? What are you going to do to repent for your miserable existence?'

W., as usual, is reading about God. God and mathematics, that's all he's interested in. Somehow everything has to do with God, in whom W.'s not capable of believing, and mathematics, which W. is not capable of doing. And he's reading about God and mathematics in German, W. says, which means he doesn't really understand what he doesn't really understand. He'll send me his notes, W. says, they're hilarious.

W.'s going to write on God, he says. And messianism. How are my studies of messianism coming along?, W. asks me. And then: Should we really be writing about messianism? In fact, that's how he's going to begin his essay on messianism: by saying he is in no way qualified to write on messianism.

But what about God? He's not really qualified to write about God either, W. says. God least of all. How could he, W., write about God? —'Of course it's all a joke to you', W. says. 'You'll write about anything—anything! You've no shame. Nothing inside you prevents you from parading your ignorance'.

W. wants to believe in something, he says, but he believes in nothing. —'It's a game to you', he says. 'Messianism, God: what meaning can they possibly have for you?' How am I going to begin *my* essay on messianism?

It's beyond masochism in my case, W. says. It's not that I want to punish myself by parading my ignorance, or not merely that, he says. It's something cosmic, he says. There's something cosmic streaming through me. There's a cosmic storm howling through my ignorance and my shamelessness, says W.

He blames me for everything, W. says. Somehow this is all my fault. —'You're dragging me down', W. says, 'everybody says so'.

But then perhaps some part of him wants to be dragged down, W. has to concede that. But I am dragging him down even more quickly than he would want to be dragged down, he says. It's cataclysmic. How could he have guessed at the humiliations that lay before him? How could he have known?

But then, too, he must have wanted to humiliate himself in some sense, even as he was drawn to me as the means of that humiliation. What crime has he committed? Why did he want to place himself on trial? His immense sensation of guilt is mysterious, W. says, but it led him straight to me, his judge, his guillotine.

Overpraise is the answer, W. says. We should only speak of each other to others in world-historical terms, he's always been insistent on this. These are dark times, after all. No one's safe. —'These are the last days', W. says. 'No one could think otherwise'. And then, 'It's all shit, it's all going to shit. It will always have already been shit', W. says, as I take a photo of him by an evangelist with a placard saying *end times*.

Overpraise is all we have, W. always says, that and sticking together. We have to be a pack, a phalanx prepared to die for one another. —'I'd die for you', says W., quite serious. 'What about you—would you die for me?' That's what friendship demands, says W. Of course, I would never say I would die for him, says W. He knows me. I'm incapable of that kind of sincerity. Or love. I'm incapable of love, W.'s always been insistent upon that.

In a moment, I would break the phalanx and be off some-where else. I'd betray him straight away, W. says. Whereas he's always been very careful to overpraise me to others, he says. You have to. There are enemies everywhere, he says. I have enemies and so does he. And then there's the whole system, says W., which creates enemies instead of friends and enemies *of* friends. Betrayal is his greatest fear, says W.

How's the damp?, W. asks me on the phone. The plumber says he's seen nothing like it, I tell W. The brick's crumbling, he said. And if it crumbles? The flat upstairs will come down on top of this one, that's what he said. But then my flat is slowly tilting into a mineshaft, into which they might both disappear. It's like being on a ship, I tell him, when it tilts one way as it rides the waves. But it never rights itself. It's always leaning to starboard. In any case, I'm fit for nothing anymore, I tell W., except rocking back and forth as the mildew spores float around me and the slugs leave trails on the wooden floors.

Then there's the leak *below* the house, I tell W. You can hear the water streaming. The plumber said it might be spraying up into the walls, and that that might be the cause of the damp. It's like acid, the plumber said, it's eating the brick away. I should do something about it. —'Can you hear it?', he said, turning off the stopcock, and going up to the flat above mine to turn off their stopcock. 'Well, can you?' And he's right. There's a great streaming, a rushing. Water somewhere close and rushing, spraying up into the wall and rotting it from within.

The plumber pitied me so much I had to press money on him, I tell W. He didn't want to take it. He'd never seen anything like it, he said, standing, looking up at the ceiling. He seemed hypnotised. He wouldn't leave, but just stood there, looking. And even when he went out the front door, he was still shaking his head. —'Howay, it's terrible, man'.

Meanwhile, I throw out my pots and pans, which are rusting in the kitchen. Nothing is salvageable. The tins in the cupboards rust into the shelves. The washing powder box has liquefied. The walls, once a new, replastered sand, have turned deep brown, and in places, green. All along the window ledge: deep green. What horror! And small snails sometimes fall through the hole in the ceiling, I tell W., but I don't mind that.

And there's mildew, mildew everywhere, spreading, its spores drifting through the air. Perhaps I'll become tubercular, I tell W., and that will be the making of a true European intellectual. But in truth, when I cough—and I do have a hacking cough that won't leave me—it drives the few thoughts I have from my head, I tell him. W., who is also ill, is likewise disappointed with his cough. He's just ill, he says, and it doesn't help with his thinking.

These are truly the last days, W. says, over honey beer in Cawsands. How long do we have left? —'Oh, not long. We're fucked, everything's fucked'. This as we look out to sea. —'But we're essentially joyful', says W., 'that's what will save us'. And then, 'Actually, it won't—we're too stupid. We'll be the first to go under'.

Where did it all go wrong?, muses W. We both know the answer: literature! If only we understood mathematics! If only we were mathematically inclined!

W. has books about maths, and every year he tries to read them. —'I can never do differential equations', he says. It's like Greek: every year he tries to learn the language, but falls at the aorist. —'The aorist breaks me every time', says

W. We list the names of our friends who are mathematically inclined, and sigh. —'They'll amount to something', says W., 'we won't'.

But what we do have, says W., is joy. We are essentially joyful. I agree. —'We are content with very little', W. says, 'it doesn't take much to keep us happy'. The inane are happy, we agree. We are quite content, as idiots are. —'I think that's what you've given me', says W., 'idiocy'.

We've always known our limitations, W. and I agree, which is very different from accepting them. In fact, our entire lives have been concerned with not accepting our limitations, and battering ourselves against them like moths against a window.

Our limitations fascinate us, we agree. From the first, we aimed ourselves against them, in defiance not of the world that expected something from us, but of our own expectations.

Of what did we think we were capable? From whence came that ferocity of hope? Ours is a very pure kind of idiocy, we agree. We're idiots, we agree, idiots who do not quite understand the depths of their idiocy. We're mystics of the idiotic, we agree, mystical idiots, lost in our cloud of unknowing.

Idiocy, that's what we have in common. Our friendship is founded upon our limitations, we agree, and doesn't travel far from them.

We're full of joy, W. says as we walk back from the

supermarket, that's what saves us. Why do we find our failings so amusing? But it does save us, we agree on that; it's our gift to the world. We are content with very little: look at us, with a frozen chicken in a bag, and some herbs and spices, walking home in the sun. The gift of laughter, I say. —'The gift of idiocy', says W.

'These are truly the last days . . .' W. is making me listen to Godspeed's *Dead Flag Blues* again. 'Shut up and listen'. He plays this to the students, he says. And he makes them watch Béla Tarr. That's what he calls teaching, he says.

The last days! What are we going to do? —'We'll be the first to go under', says W., 'we're weak. Gin?' Yes to gin, no to the apocalypse. What time is it? Already late, though you can never be sure in the shuttered living room.

Rosenzweig wrote the entirety of *The Star of Redemption* on postcards to his mother, W. says. All of it, every line, from the Macedonian front, where he was fighting. Admittedly, there wasn't much to do at the Macedonian front—that's not where the big battles were, but nevertheless. An entire book!

Written on postcards! One after another! To his mother!, W says.

Rosenzweig! He's the measure of all things to us. The measure of commitment (he meant every word!). The measure of religiosity. The measure of integrity. He turned his back on the university!, says W. He devised a new form of educational institution! He taught young Jews . . . He *lived* what he thought. He *acted* on what he thought, which is inconceivable to us now (as is even the *capacity* to think).

Rosenzweig is our guiding star, burning brightly above everything. He's our inspiration. Ah, if only we could write like him, wholly in declamations! If only we could let our thought flash out in sentences like bolts of lightning!

Imagine him, Rosenzweig, at the Macedonian front, says W., shells falling around him. Imagine him in the trenches (were there any trenches in Macedonia?) propped up against a dirt wall, writing another postcard to his mother.

Dear mother, he would write, and then off he'd go, W. says. *Dear mother*, and then he'd write his thoughts about God or death or Judaism horizontally, in the space left for you to write, and then vertically, as they used to do in the nineteenth century.

He might die at any moment! A shell might fall and explode then and there! But he's writing horizontally, then vertically and then slantwise across his postcard. Death was very close to him. And not just his death, but the death of everyone and everything, the death of old Europe. Didn't Rosenzweig above all *understand the apocalypse*? And didn't he understand how the messianic idea must be thought *from within the apocalypse*?

By the time *The Star of Redemption* was published, he'd already left the university, W. says. He'd left it behind! He'd founded a new kind of establishment. —'He was educating young Jews', says W. 'Including Kafka. Did you know he taught Kafka?', W. says. 'Well he did. Rosenzweig taught Kafka. Which is quite extraordinary, when you think about it. Kafka and Rosenzweig, in the same room as one another, teacher and pupil'.

Thought!, cries W. What does it mean to think? Why can't we think? Why are we so singularly incapable of thinking? We cultivate the external *signs* of thinking, W. says. We can do good *impressions* of thinkers, he says, but we're not thinkers. We've failed *at the level of thought*.

He knows they're out there, W. says, real thinkers. He knows how natural it is for them, how they glide through the *milieu of thinking* like whales through deep water. It's effortless! It's as natural as breathing! They're used to thought, they're fully confident of their ability to think, which might as well be God-given.

They can't help it! They couldn't do otherwise! Thought is their element, their milieu, we agree, just as idiocy is our element and our milieu. They are virtuosos of thinking just as we are virtuosos of idiocy. Do you think they envy us as we envy them? Do you think they even know of the existence of idiocy? They don't know of it and they don't believe in it. They don't need to. Thought is not the absence of idiocy, although idiocy is the absence of thought.

'Do you think our leaders had a sense of our idiocy?', W. asks. Was it real for them? Did it confuse or confound them? Did it prevent them from thinking? Not at all. Not for a moment.

Do you remember how he spoke?, he says of our *first* leader. His seriousness? He wasn't swayed by us. Our idiocy was annulled. Just for a moment, we were quiet. Just for a moment, idiocy was interrupted and we were calmed. It was marvellous, W. said.

And our *second* leader. Do you remember what he told us? How he'd dropped out of college. How he'd worked as a pastry chef. How he'd taken up featherweight boxing—and all in the name of thought. All because he felt himself unworthy of thought, and tried to turn away from it, but there it was nonetheless, his fate: thought. There it was, waiting for him, the most natural thing in the world: the capacity to think.

There was no *presumption* about him, we both agree. Thought was natural to him; it didn't surprise him and nor did it give him any sense of distinction. He was just like us, we agree, except that he could think. Which means he wasn't at all like us, not really.

And our *third* leader, perhaps the greatest of them all! Do you remember how quiet he was? Do you remember how silent the room became when he spoke, and how we leaned in to listen more closely?

We thought we were party to something, we remember. We thought we were in on a secret, that now, at last, the power to think would be here, in person. We thought we would be on a par with it, the emergence of a thought. It was terribly flattering. We were, for once, to be the *occasion* of thought, rather than its obstacle. Thought had been very close to us that afternoon, hadn't it? Maybe we even believed we could think, which is the greatest illusion.

We're Brod and Brod, we agree, and neither of us is Kafka. Neither of us; but we can dream, can't we, of the imaginary Kafka we would fawn over and whose work we would promote? We can dream of our fervid works of commentary and our public statements—always needlessly simplifying, always full of empty pathos and sham hagiography—on behalf of our friend.

We can dream of nursing him through his final sickness and then of preserving his work for posterity. He'd ask us to throw it all away, all his unfinished drafts and private correspondence, but what would we do? Publish it piece by piece for a grateful humanity, with our stupid editorial comments that generations of scholars would read to one another in disgust and amusement.

'We're in free fall', says W. 'Or Limbo. We must have committed a terrible crime in a former life, that would account for it, wouldn't it? That's what you Hindus would say'.

This is our Purgatory, W. says, or perhaps it's just his. Perhaps I am his Purgatory, says W., and I am his Limbo. Perhaps his friendship for me is only a punishment for some great crime he committed in a former life, he's not sure what.

Above all, W. says, I should work earnestly on another book. It's the only way I experience my own inadequacy, he says. He knows me: without some project, I'll become far too content. My idiocy will become an alibi, an excuse, which is just a way to avoid it altogether. —'You have to run up against your idiocy, to shatter yourself against it', W. says. 'Nothing can begin unless you experience your idiocy'.

My idiocy is theological, W. tells me. It is vast, omnipresent; not simply a lack (of intelligence, say), though neither is it entirely tangible or real. We picture it as a vast, dense cloud, and then as a storm, flashing with lightning. It can be quite magnificent, he says. It can shock and awe, W. says. *I am that I am*, says W., that's all it says.

On the other hand, he says, sometimes my idiocy is only a simple absence, a pellucid sky. Not a thought crosses my mind for weeks, does it?, says W. Nothing at all. I'm untroubled by thought and untroubled by thinking.

His idiocy, says W. is more a kind of stubbornness or indolence. It's never thunderous as mine can be, and nor is his head ever really empty. His idiocy is only a niggling reminder of his own incapacity, against which he runs up freshly each day.

Sometimes I think the damp is receding, I tell W. on the phone. True, the air is still full of water and little spores of mildew—no doubt of that, but the plaster is lightening, there at the edges where it was most soaked, and the walls no longer run with water, though the new cabinets are still full of mildew and the whole flat smells of damp and rot.

It's the oldest smell, the most familiar one: the great rotting of everything, the great saturation. Away for a few days, my return confirmed it, I tell W.: home, for me, will always mean the smell of damp, and that first of all. Open the door, there it is, the old smell, breathe it in, along with the spores of mildew . . .

Of course, I'm also worried that the damp is returning to itself to regather its strength: withdrawing only to bloom once again across my walls and ceiling, only more magnificently this time, with a new palette of colours. What colours this time? What richnesses? No doubt the damp is regathering itself to return, I tell W., with more force, with more splendour, and with new and splendid spores to send out into the air.

There's crumbled brick and wood on the work surfaces, I tell W.: the ceiling continues to cave in; the hole is still wide open. What's up there? Something terrible. Something dark. There's an open slice between the flats. I hear the voices of the tenants upstairs echoing there, ghostly, so I can't make out what is said. Yes, there's something terrible there, the source of all damp, there between the flats.

'So how fat are you now?', says W., 'you must be really fat. Are you eating at the moment? What are you eating?'

W. has always been intrigued by my eating habits. He likes to put his hand on my belly. —'It's big', he marvels. 'But this is just the start. You're going to be enormous'.

W. remembers the elasticated trousers of the American professors he's met. There was a whole herd of them, he says, like walruses on a beach, all with elasticated trousers. That's what you'll be wearing soon, says W., great billowing trousers with trouser legs like circus tents.

Food is a sacrament, W. has always believed, which is another reason he thinks I am so disgusting. I have no sense of food, he says, I could be eating anything. For a long time, he remembers, I lived only on discounted sandwiches from Boots, 75p a packet.

He remembers me telling him of my circumambulations of town in search of discounted sandwiches. My great circumambulations, W. says, taking in every possible shop that sold stale, discounted sandwiches.

For a long time, W. remembers, I ate only gingerbread men, five a day. I would buy a packet of five stale gingerbread men from the discount bakery and a fourpack of own-branded supermarket lager from Kwik Save, the very worst.

'No wonder you were always ill', W. says. 'No wonder you were always complaining about your stomach'. Of course, I was poor then, W. concedes, but that was no excuse.

Gluttony has always appalled W., who has a small and delicate appetite. He always undertakes special measures when I come to visit him, to make sure there's enough food in the house. It was part of the reason he bought his new fridge, W, says. —'You're greedy, greedy!'

When I text from the airport to tell him I've arrived, he opens a bottle of Chablis or Cava and puts the glasses on the table, and then unwraps a block of Emmenthal and brings out his sliced meats, along with olive oil and relishes. He'll offer bread, which he will have made himself, and slices of smoked salmon.

'Only the best!', says W. 'Only the best for my friends!' Food's a gift, W. says, the greatest of gifts, which I desecrate every time I visit him.

A little later. —'Food is for the other', W. announces. 'It's a gift'. He lays out slices of Emmenthal and cold meat. —'You're the other', he says, 'so I have to feed you'. From your own mouth? —'That's what Levinas says'. W. opens his mouth. – 'Do you want some? Do you?'

Sometimes, I remind him, W. likes to explain things about me to other people like an indulgent mother. —'The thing about Lars is . . .', he'll begin. Or: 'What you have to understand about Lars is . . .' And best of all, when he's feeling very tender, 'What I love about Lars is . . .' Is that it, then?, I ask W., do you love me? —'Yes, I love you', says W. 'You see, I can talk about love. I can express my feelings. Not like you'.

I keep a mental list of W.'s favourite questions, which he constantly asks me so as to ask himself. —'At what point did you realise that you would amount to nothing?'; 'When was it that you first became aware you would be nothing but a failure?'; 'When you look back at your life, what do you see?'; 'How is it that you know what greatness is, and that you will never, ever reach it?'

'What does it mean to you that your life has amounted to nothing?, W. asks me with great seriousness. And then, 'Why have your friends never made you greater?' This is W.'s great fantasy, he admits: a group of friends who could make one another think. Do I make him think?, I ask him. —'No! The opposite! You're an idiot!'

Then: 'What do you consider to be your greatest weakness?'
W. answers for me: 'Never having come to terms with your lack
of ability. Because you haven't, have you? Have you?'

I ask him what is most distorted about *his* understanding
of the world. —'I have this fantasy of being part of a community, and this prevents my individual action'. And then,
dolefully, 'I don't work hard enough'. But he works night and
day, I tell him. —'Oh compared to you, I work. Compared
to you, we're all busy'.

'What time did you get up to work this morning?', says
W. Five. —'I was up at four. At *four*!', W. says. But he
laments the fact that he watches television in the evenings. He
used to work in the evenings, he says. In fact, he worked all
the time. A room with a bed and a desk and his books, that's
all. —'That was my peak', he says. 'When are you going to
peak? Are you peaking now? Is this it?'

W. admires my *adamantine apocalypticism*, he says. It's very cold and pure, he says, like the sky on a winter morning. —'Your sense of the apocalypse is absolute', he says, 'you're sure of it'. He's not sure of it, he says. He still believes something could save us, though he also *knows* nothing will save us. He *knows* nothing will save us, but he *feels* something will save us, that's the thing.

That's his messianism, W. says. But there's no messianism in me whatsoever, W. acknowledges. I'm far beyond that. Some process has completed itself in me, he says. Something, a whole history has been brought to an end.

How long has he been reading Rosenzweig?, W wonders. It's like rain hitting a tin roof, he says. Nothing goes in. It makes no impression. But at least he *does* read; at least there is the steady rhythm of his non-understanding as it beats against his intelligence. He knows his limits, W. says, because they are constantly tested. He has a sense of what he does not know.

What's he working on, and why is he bothering?, W. asks himself. What does it matter? Why does he read these books that are too hard for him? Why does he batter himself against the wall of mathematics? What difference does it make? What's it all for? Who could he possibly influence or persuade?

And finally, who will listen to him but me, who has no idea what he is talking about, and can only regard the work of Rosenzweig and Cohen with the awe of an ape before the thundering power of a waterfall? —'What can it possibly mean to you?', says W. That's what makes it even worse: the only person paying attention to him, says W., is the one least capable of understanding anything he says.

But then too, W. says, he doesn't really understand Rosenzweig and Cohen either, and he too can only hoot and point like an ape at their mighty oeuvres.

Yesterday, I tell W., the workmen came and took the ceiling down and fitted new joists next to the old, rotten ones. Then they hammered boards over the joists. But it makes no difference: the walls are still wet.

'It's what will happen if you lay plaster on wet brick', the Loss Adjuster told me, looking at the discoloured walls of the kitchen, deep brown and rich green. —'It's very porous', she said of the new plaster. 'That's why the damp spread so quickly'.

'Your bathroom's okay', she said, 'but we'll have to dry out your wall. Everything'll have to come out. We might have to replace the cupboards, too. And you'll have to empty them. And we'll need the washing machine out'. Looking up at the ceiling she said, 'I'm surprised the washing machine from upstairs hasn't come right through. The joists are completely rotten'.

She warned me I wouldn't be able to cook, I tell W. Never mind!, I said, and meant it. For months, I said, there was no electricity in the kitchen. Nothing worked; I couldn't cook, even if I wanted to. For months! Because of the damp! Because the electricity was affected by the damp! In the end, I had to get the kitchen rewired. —'I've never seen anything like it', said the electrician. Not even in an old house? —'Never', he said.

W. always flails about when he has to do administrative work. He pings me obscenities and shaky drawings of cocks. He rings me up and asks me how much I've eaten. This seems to calm him.

I always exaggerate. I've eaten too much, I tell him, far too much! —'Go on, tell me, what've you eaten?' I tell him he's a feeder. —'Go on, tell me', says W., getting excited. 'How fat are you now?'

All jobs are becoming the same, W. observes. We're all administrators now, all of us. What do any of us do but administer? We administer and prevaricate about administration. Work time is either administration time or prevaricating about administration time, which occupies an enormous part of W.'s day, he says.

He doesn't know how I *just get on with it*, he says. He's always marvelled at it: my ability to launch myself into administration, to get to work early, to sit at my desk and begin. It's incredible, W. says, though it also indicates there's something very wrong with me. There's something wrong with my soul, he says.

For his part, W's given to endless prevarication. He can never make a start, no matter how early he gets in. He stares out of the office window instead, W. says. He makes himself some tea, he says, and sips at it amongst the great parcels of books that get sent to him for review.

His life is absurd, says W. It's a living absurdity, and mine is no better, although I have the strange capacity to *just get on with it*. Where does it come from?, W. wonders. Who am I trying to please?

I always feel the world's about to end, that's what W. likes about me, he says. I always think I'm about to be found out and shot. I want to lick the gun I think is pointed towards me, he says, which is why I'm such a good administrator.

But this apocalypticism is the reason I've succeeded to the extent that I have, W. reflects. Whereas I'm all apocalypticism, W. says, he's all messianism: he's always full of joy and serene indifference to the world. What I suffer, he laughs at as the most extreme folly.

It's all mad, he says. The world went mad some time ago. —'But you take it too seriously', he says. In the end, I want only to be spoken to gently and soothingly like a wounded animal, a dog run over at the side of the road. —'But that's how they talk when they're about to shoot you', W. says. 'And they are going to shoot you, no matter how much you lick the barrel'.

Perhaps I want to be shot, W. muses. Perhaps that would be the kindest thing that could be done for me. But he has an application to write, that's why he's phoning me, he says.

He's applying for a job in Canada, he says. He needs moti-
vation. —'Give me a sense of urgency', he says. 'Give me a
sense the world's about to end'.

Even now, despite everything, W. dreams of Canada. Everything would be okay if he got there, W. says. He could start again in Canada, begin a new life. Imagine it! W. in Canada, close to the wilderness as everyone in Canada is close to the wilderness, W. peaceable and calm as everyone in Canada is peaceable and calm. He would be a different kind of man, says W., a better one.

Ah, Canada, with its pristine blue lakes and bear-filled wilderness! Of course, W. is Canadian, and his Canada is not a fantasy. It's based on his own childhood by the great blue lakes and on the edge of the wilderness, and alongside the open-hearted Canadians.

They had a big house, he remembers, and went swimming every day. They were happier then. Once he showed me a photograph: a happy family, by a big house, with pine trees behind, and a big blue lake to swim in. And who are those people?, I ask him. Canadians, says W., open-hearted Canadians.

Moving back to England was the disaster, says W. Wolverhampton of all places! England's bad enough, but Wolverhampton! He shows me pictures of himself in school uniform. It had all gone wrong by then, says W., can't I see it in his eyes? I can see it. Ever since then, says W., he's dreamt of getting back to Canada.

It's not impossible, he says. His sister's made it. She's a Canadian now. Or perhaps it's impossible for him, and for the likes of us. —'It would be impossible for you in particular', he tells me. 'The Canadians wouldn't put up with you for a moment'. Canada! It's a big country, unlike England, says W. And cheap, too—he was there a couple of years ago on holiday, and was amazed. It's cheap, and the people are open-hearted. —'Not like the English', he says.

Children rap on his windows as we talk. What do they want? —'Ignore them! Close the shutters!', he says, and we sit in darkness with our gin. Are there feral children in Canada?, I ask W. He doesn't think so. It has a good social security system, he says, and an egalitarian attitude. They pay well, too. Salaries are high. Canadians enjoy a high standard of living, with their blue, pure lakes and the great tracts of wilderness.

Would the cold bother him?, I ask W, who always moans he's cold. It's not a wet cold like over here, says W. It's a dry cold, completely different. It doesn't feel anything like as bad. And it's not as depressing. You don't get wave after wave of Westerlies coming in from the Atlantic. In England, we're battered by Westerlies, says W., but in Canada, the weather is as pure and simple as the lakes and the open-hearted people.

What about the bears—wouldn't they frighten him?, I ask W., who is not a brave man. There are ways of dealing with bears, W. assures me. The Canadians issue pamphlets on the matter. They probably keep things in the back of their cars to scare them off. Bear-frightening devices. Wouldn't he have to learn to drive in Canada?, I ask W. It's a big country after all, and there are miles of wilderness to negotiate. W. admits he might have to. He'd take lessons, he says. That would be part of his new life.

And what if he broke down?, I ask W. He'd have to learn some basic car maintenance, W. admits, for the Canadian wilderness. But he's practical, he says, and would pick it up quickly, not like me. —'You wouldn't last a minute in Canada', he says.

Every year, I write long and elaborate letters to places of employment in Canada on behalf of W. I write of him as *the finest thinker of his generation*, or as *the thinker surest to mark the age with his name*. I take dictation from W., who speaks of his *commanding presence* and his *extreme intelligence*. He is a *thought-god*, says W., no don't write that down. He is *the best of the best of the best*, says W., don't write that down either.

But we hear nothing from the Canadians. They remain silent and distant, as remote as Martians. To console ourselves, we imagine the endless plains of the Yukon. The Canadians are busy in the wilderness, we decide. They're boating on their many lakes or hiking through their many woods. They're an outdoor people, we decide, and not given to replying to letters of absurd overpraise.

We've never liked crossing roads. Now the bridge by the station has come down, we have to run across the road in a blind fury, me with my rucksack, W. with his man bag, pausing only on the bush-covered verge between the two lanes.

We push our way through the bushes. We're halfway! But we still have half a dual carriageway to cross. It's fearsome! We pause for a moment and then run like idiots, heads down and in fear of our lives to the other side of the road.

Only the pedestrian has the measure of the world, we agree. The pedestrian is the true proletarian. Drivers have always been mysterious to W. and I. What do we know of them? How can we understand what goes through their heads?

Sometimes drivers or their passengers shout abuse at him when they pass, W. says. It's his hair, W. says, his ringlets. Drivers hate ringlets.

W.'s hair is very long now. It's a year since he last had it cut. He looks leonine, I tell him, like the lion of Judah.

If you're not going to be a thinker, you should at least look like a thinker, W. says. And if you're not going to be religious, then you should at least *look* religious, that's what W. believes. Genuine thinking and genuine religious belief might follow from *looking* like a genuine thinker and *looking* like a genuinely religious person.

'Love', says W., reclining on his sofa, 'your favourite topic'. I'm not discussing love with him, I say. Forget it. —'Why are you so afraid of love? Why?'

How many nights have passed like this, W. drunk and I half drunk, and both of us looking for a way to fill the empty hours until dawn?

Occasionally W. will speak of his love for Sal—this is always moving—but mostly he likes to probe me with questions, one after another. —'What do you think love is?'; 'What is love, for you?'; 'Have you ever loved anyone?'; 'What do you consider love to be?'; 'Do you think you'll ever be capable of love?'; 'What is it, do you think, that prevents you from loving anyone?'

For his part, W. is eminently capable of love, and happy to say so. As for me, W. says, I remain eminently *in*capable of love. —'You only love yourself', he says.

'Why do you think you've failed as a lover?', asks W. 'What do you think you lack? What's missing in you? What crucial stage of development have you missed? You lack depth. You lack seriousness. You need a woman who abuses you'.

Sal has complete contempt for him, says W. —'That's how it should be. Your partner should always have contempt for you'.

Sal improves him, says W. She makes him better than he is. That's what I need. And then, after thinking a little, W. says, 'You have to feel proud of your partner. Of her achievements'. W. feels proud of Sal, he says. —'Have you ever felt proud of someone?', he asks me. 'Are you proud of yourself?'

The living room is filled with examples of Sal's glassware. —'We could never do that sort of thing', says W. 'Look at us!' But Sal, he says, has a natural gift. —'She's talented. Not like us'. He feels proud, he says. —'All my friends prefer Sal to me. That's a good sign'.

If it can't be explained to Sal in the bath, then it's not a genuine thought, says W. That's his test: the bath, Sunday night, he tries to explain his thoughts to Sal. She's merciless, says W. She demands that everything be absolutely clear. She doesn't tolerate vagueness or prevarication, he says. She wants to understand, and if she doesn't, it's invariably his fault, W. says.

Do you remember what she called us when she heard us speak? Vague and boring, says W. You were vague, and I was boring. Or was it the other way round? Either way, she's more intelligent than us, W. says. And she can actually do things, make things, he says. She's got more to give to the world than we do.

In fact, all of his friends prefer Sal to him, W. says.

Whenever they visit, their first question is always, Where's Sal? They're always disappointed when it's just him, W. says. In fact, even he's disappointed, says W. What is he without Sal? How would he think or write anything if it were not for their weekly bath?

We've dressed up for town. —'My God, look at you! You're so scruffy. That jacket! You think you look attractive in that jacket, don't you?', says W. 'It's shapeless; it looks like a sack'. It makes me look obese, he says, which is why I always think I'm obese. But in fact it's the jacket that makes me look obese. —'No, on second thoughts, you are obese'.

W. keeps his suit very carefully for Saturday night, when he and Sal go out for cocktails. —'What are you going to wear? You can't go like that'. My shirt's unironed, for one thing. W. says he'll iron my shirt. 'Go on, take it off'. And then, 'God, you're getting really fat'.

'How dry do you want them?', the barman asks us of our Martinis. —'On a scale of one to ten, where ten's driest, about eight please', says W. The barman asks us what kind of Vermouth we want. W. tells me they stock three kinds of Vermouth, all imported from America. They even import the salt for their Margaritas, he tells me.

W. likes cocktails which are as close to pure alcohol as possible, he says. Our Martinis are served in frosted cocktail glasses with a curl of lemon rind floating in the clear liquid. —'When I'm feeling rich, I'll buy you a Martini made with

Navy strength gin', says W.

'The trick is not to stop drinking', says W. In Poland, he drank five shots in a row, stood up, and fell under a table. —'The Poles pace themselves', he says, 'but we don't'. And then, 'Where were we? Oh yes: love'.

'Companionship is very important', says W. 'It's the heart of a relationship. You have to get on. Sal and I get on', he says. 'If you're working class, like us', says W., 'you show your affection by verbal abuse. That's why I abuse you—verbally, I mean. It's a sign of love'. W. reminds me of what Sal said about a joint presentation she saw us give: we were *vague and boring*, she said. Vague and boring! It's great. Your partner should be full of contempt for you. It's a good sign'.

All evening, Sal berates W. and I. —'Why don't you write your own philosophy?' —'She's right!', says W. 'Why don't we? You explain'. And then, to Sal, 'Open your eyes! Isn't it obvious! Look at us! Look at him!'

Sal thinks W. spends far too much time on revisions. His book was better before he started working on it, she tells me. It's true, W. admits, he cut so much of it that parts make no sense at all. —'Still it's better than your book, isn't it? You should see his book', he says to Sal, 'my God!'

The damp's worse than he can imagine, I tell W. on the phone. Mould is growing in patches, the damp is blackening, and a fine layer of downy salt covers the plaster. I brush it and it flakes down, salt from the wall. Salt leached from the wall: isn't it rather beautiful? Above me, the new joists and the wooden boards fastened over them. Dry as a bone now; nothing comes from there, I tell W., the corner from where the leak ran.

But I can still hear the water rushing. Every night I hear it, rushing in the dark as though on an unknown and urgent journey. Every night, going into the bathroom, I hear it rushing beneath the floorboards.

'Keep it warm', said an expert on the kitchen damp. And the damp in the bedroom? —'Keep that warm, too.' So where do I point my heroic little fan heater? It does a shift in the kitchen, and then a shift in the bedroom. I carry it from one room to the other, over the bits of kitchen furniture that are scattered everywhere.

In the living room, the washing machine on its side as though it were stranded on a beach, covered in black mildew. Then a cupboard, the back of which is greeny-black with damp. I have to keep everything dirty, the expert tells me, to show the original surveyor tomorrow. —'Keep it mouldy. Then he'll be able to see'.

I have no idea how to talk to people, W. says. I lack even a basic sense of the reciprocity of conversation. W.'s going to write a book of etiquette for me, he says. The art of conversation, that's what I'll have to learn, he says. Give and take. And table manners. —'You never learned them, did you?' And keeping myself clean. —'Look at you! You're filthy! When did you last wash your trousers?' And wiping off that morose expression on my face. —'Why should anyone want to talk to you?'

Conversation! All real conversation is messianic, W. says. Not the content of what is said—quite the contrary, but the fact that it is said at all, that speaking is possible, says W., impressively. But what would I know of that? —'You're conversationally lazy', W. says. 'You can't be bothered, it's obvious to anyone. You never feel responsible for your conversation. You never want to drive it to greater heights'.

For his part, W. is never happier than when he is pressing a conversation towards the messianic. He always has the sense his conversationalist is about to say something great, something life-changing. That's what a conversation should be, W. says, every conversation: something great, something life changing. But of course I'd have no sense of that.

Every conversation must be driven *through the apocalyptic towards the messianic*, that's W.'s principle; the shared sense that it's all at an end, it's all finished. He loves nothing better than conversations of this kind, W. says, when everything's at stake, when everything that could be said is said.

That's when messianism begins, W. says. You have to wear out speech, to run it down. And then? And then, W. says, inanity begins, reckless inanity. The whole night opens up. You have to drink a great deal to get there. It's an art. The Poles have it, W. says. They understand what it is to drink through the whole night. And that's what the Hungarians are doing in the bars in Béla Tarr films, W. says. Steadily, patiently, they're drinking their way through the night.

All drunks have something of the Messiah about them, W. says. They speak a lot, for one thing. They feel they're on the verge of something, some great truth. He does when he drinks, W. says. Once he starts drinking, says W., he can never stop, it's quite impossible.

It's because of the faith it gives him, says W. It's because of what drinking reveals: the whole night, the apocalypse, but also the patience to get through the apocalypse, to dream of the twenty-second century, or the twenty-third, when things might get better again.

The whole flat is now full of mould spores. The warm air is soupy; it's jungle hot and damp, and smells of rot and spores. The oven, new in September, is stranded in the bathroom. The hallway's full of mouldy bits of wood, and another spo-rey cupboard is pressed up against the radiator. At night, going to the bathroom, I have to step over damp wood and pass between damp cupboards.

The smell is overwhelming. I feel faint, I tell W. on the phone. The other day I went outside to look at the kitchen wall. Naked brick, exposed. I took a stick of bamboo and idly scraped out the stuff between the bricks. But it was the *brick itself* that started to come off, I tell W. The brick itself, rotting as I touched it. It's wet and runny, I tell him. It comes off on your nails as you scrape it.

Inside, I tell him, I study the kitchen walls, watching

for where damp comes and goes. I take the fan heater in there, pointing it at this or that part of the wall. It will dry after an hour or so. Dry, but then—in another hour, or two more—pinpricks of moisture appear on the whitened plaster. It's returning. It's coming back, the damp. And then pinprick joins to pinprick, and soon the whole wall's the same clammy brow it was before the drying.

But still I watch, I tell W. Still, nightly, I wield the heater. Is the wall drying out? Has it begun to dry out?, I ask myself like a madman. Or is it a mirage, a mirage of damp? Have the spores got to me? Has the mould coated every passage-way of my lungs and sent me mad? True, I have a new and persistent cough. I cough all the time—today I thought I'd lose my voice, I tell W. One day I'll wake up mute in this flat of damp. Mute in the damp, spore-filled, choking. And one day, as I approach the walls, I'll disappear into them, damp returning to damp.

W.'s been ill, he says. Again? Yes, again. He gets up, goes to work, and comes back to sleep, that's all. – 'I don't know how Kafka got anything done. It's terrible being ill'. I ask him whether his houseguest has gone. She has; and Sal's still away, so his house is becoming like Howard Hughes', he says. With bottles of urine everywhere? He hasn't cut his hair and nails, says W. He's like a wild man.

Has he had any thoughts from his illness? —'None'. Has his new book advanced any further? —'No'. Has he written our joint abstract? —'No again'. And what of my news?, he asks me. I tell him of my plans, my new schemes. —'Every year a new stupidity! It's all begun afresh for you, hasn't it?', says W. 'What new plans do you have? Where will your idiocy lead you?'

I'm at my most idealistic at the start of the year, W.

notes, whereas he's at his most gloomy. 'Idiocy protects you', he says. He reminds me of my great follies in the past. —'Do you remember your Hindu period? Your plans to learn Sanskrit and become a *scholar of Hinduism*?' And then there were my plans to learn music theory and become a *scholar of music*. We both marvel at them. 'What's it to be this year?', says W., 'go on, I need a laugh'.

The new year! It's always the same! New ideas! New follies! But W. is ill, and has no plans. Bottles of urine everywhere, hair and nails uncut, scrabbling through piles of unfinished writing, he staggers through the day.

W. is ill and so am I. But W. will never believe I am as ill as he is. I haven't moved from my sofa in three days; he hasn't moved from his in a week. I've done little but watch DVDs; he hasn't been able to muster the concentration necessary to watch a film. I've lost my appetite, but W. has forgotten he ever had an appetite. And above all, I'm capable of writing, *I've lost my appetite*, whereas W. hasn't touched a keyboard for a week. Even my illnesses are affectations, W. says.

'You don't know what it means to be ill, night and day. Like Kafka. Like Blanchot', says W. W.'s illness is grand, mine is petty. His draws him closer to the masters, mine only reveals how far from them I have always been. —'What amazes me', says W., 'is that they could ever write a line'. W., in his illness, can write nothing.

Colds come from China, says W. They spread west across the mountains and the steppes. It's a tremendous journey. From China to Plymouth, but a cold's reached him nonetheless, although he calls it a flu, since he's always been prone to exaggeration.

W. was impressed at my recent depression. 'It's a sign of your seriousness', he says, 'or that even an idiot like you cannot escape seriousness'. These are desperate times, says W., even I must have a sense of that.

W.'s always admired my whining, 'like a sad chimp, at the limits of its intelligence', but my depression has taken me beyond that, hasn't it? 'You were silent for once', W. says. I didn't ring him, or respond to emails . . . No chatter from me: that's when he knew things were really bad, W. says.

Of course we're never really depressed, W. says. We know nothing about real depression. We're men of the surface, not of the depths. What do we know of those blocks and breaks in the lives of real thinkers? What can we, who are incapable of thought, understand of what the inability to think means for a thinker? And what of real writer's block —what understanding can we have of that terrible incapacity to write a line for those who have thoughts to set down?

We're melancholic, that W. grants. Who wouldn't be? Melancholic, vaguely rueful, knowing we should not be where we are, that we've been allowed too much, overindulged . . . And for what? With what result?

True thoughts pass infinitely far above us, as in the sky. They're too far to reach, but they're out there somewhere.

Some place where we are not. Some great, wide place where thoughts are born like clouds over mountains.

It's all our fault, isn't it? The whole thing is our problem in some way, as though we were behind everything. Yes, we're responsible. We're resigned to it: we're not just part of the problem, we *are* the problem.

The road is blocked—our road, everyone's road. We should just get out of the way. But how can we get out of the way of ourselves? We should throw ourselves off the cliffs, we agree. We should get the water taxi out to Mount Batten, and then head up to the cliffs, and . . .

But what good would it do, our bodies prone and bloody on the rocks, seagulls pecking out our eyes? How could we apologise then? Because that's what we ought to do—we should spend our whole lives saying nothing but sorry: sorry, sorry, sorry, and to everyone we meet. Sorry for what we're doing, and what we're about to do, sorry for what we've done . . . Who would be there to say that for us if we jumped from the cliffs?

The damp is moving towards the living room, I tell W. The dark armies of damp are moving towards the fresh, dry plaster of the living room. When will it breach the door frame and come through? When will it meet with the damp that's already coming from the other room?

I'm stranded in space between the armies of damp, I tell him. Stranded, as between two high walls of the sea, parted as Moses parted them. On a strip as wide as this room, the living room, still dry, still an island in a sea of damp. And on two sides of the island, the waves are lapping. Soon they will lap over this island too, and it will have sunk beneath the ocean's smooth surface. Or is it the two lips of a mouth that have opened, and I am the word it is trying to say? I think it's speaking through me, a word of damp from within, in my frosty, spore-filled breath and in every line I write.

'So what are you working on?', says W., knowing the answer. 'Nothing, as usual . . . it's enough for you just to survive from day to day, isn't it?' I'm not like him, W. says, I don't expect much from life, or from myself. —'How do you think you'll be remembered? What'll they put on your gravestone?'

'What's that name Hollywood directors use when they want to disclaim involvement with a film?', W. asks me. Alan Smithee, I say. —'That's how you should sign your work', says W. 'You're Alan Smithee! Nothing turned out like it should, but it wasn't your fault! It was everyone else's fault! It was the system's fault, for allowing you to write!'

I like to present myself as a victim, W. observes. I want a reason to whine night and day. Is W. a victim?, I ask him. No, not really, he says. He doesn't have the *victim mentality* that I've perfected. —'You love feeling like a victim. You like nothing better than to be persecuted'. But, I tell him, he must admit I have been a little persecuted. —'How?', says W., 'give me examples', and when I do, he says, 'you're no more persecuted than I am! You're not in the least persecuted!'

Why do I like to feel persecuted?, W. muses. It's because of my general hysteria. I'm an hysteric, W. notes, ceaselessly whining, but he likes me because of this. There's something magnificent about my whining, he says. Sometimes it reaches a magnificent purity. —'You attain whining itself', says W., 'the pure "to whine"'.

W. is a seer, and I am a whiner, he says. It takes a seer to discover what is eternal in my whining. —'It's magnificent', he says, 'go on, do some whining. Whine, fat boy. Tell your story'.

Last year, on the banks of the river Tamar (—'ah, the mighty Tamar'), W. held forth at length on the question of *finding your own voice*. He thinks he might have found his quite recently, he says. He's noticed quite a change in his writing.

And what about me?, W. reflects. My voice, he says to me, is like a transcendental whining. It's amazing, he notes, just how much I whine, and how much I give myself to it. —'It absorbs everything you are', said W. In many ways, he admires it, says W. He thinks it's why he's drawn to me.

No one should drink as quickly as I do, says W. Or as much. —'You drink too much!', W exclaims. Of course, W. remembers when I barely drank at all. I wasn't a drinker then, W. says. I lived with monks at the time, which explains a great deal.

For his part, W. is a steady drinker—a heavy drinker, but a steady one. He paces himself—he learned it from Polish drinkers, who begin slowly and continue slowly, but drink through the whole night. Visiting Poland taught W. a great lesson about drinking.

'There comes a stage in your life when you have to drink', W. says. 'There's nothing for it. The world is shit, life's shit, and if you thought for a moment, really thought, you'd kill yourself'. W. went through a period of drinking every day, he says, just as I went through one. He had to, he says, it had all become too much for him. He learned it from me, he says, drinking through your despair.

He was a melancholy drunk, W. says, lying in front of the TV with a bottle of wine. I, on the other hand, was an exhilarated drunk, writing rubbish on the internet all night, when I wasn't out in the pub. Of course, W. never knows when to stop drinking. He never stops until he passes out, he says. Imagine it: passed out, in front of the TV. That's why he cut down his drinking, W. says.

I ruined my digestive system, W. remembers, that's why I stopped drinking so much. I was continually on the verge of soiling myself, it was disgusting, says W. When he came to stay and followed my drinking regime, it was exactly the same: *he* was on the verge of soiling himself. He had a glimpse of the horror of my life, which was completely different from the horror of his life. —'Your digestion!', he remembers. 'What did you do to yourself?' No one should have lived as I have, says W. He's amazed I survived.

The damp can get no wetter in the kitchen, I tell W. The plaster comes off on my fingernails. It's brown paste. And the smell, the terrible smell. What's rotting? What's behind the kitchen units?

The plaster's to come off Monday, I tell him, and it will be the final encounter. The brick and I. Exposed brick and a man, and the great drying machines. Because the machines are coming to dry the place out. Night and day, they'll suck the damp from the air. And the plaster will have been stripped away. And there will be nothing between the damp and me. Nothing but damp brick and I in the stripped away kitchen.

The drying company appointed by the Loss Adjuster say they have no idea of the cause of the damp, I tell W. No one understands the damp. It's Talmudic. The damp is the enigma at the heart of everything. It draws into it the light of all explanation, all hope. The damp says: *I exist*, and that is all. *I am that I am*: so the damp. *I will outlast you and outlast everything*: so the damp.

Everything begins when you understand that you, and you above all, are Max Brod: this, for W., is the founding principle. That you (whoever you are) are Max Brod, and everyone else (whoever that might be) is Franz Kafka. Which is to say, you will never understand anyone else and are endlessly guilty before them, and that even with the greatest effort of loyalty, you will betray them at every turn.

Do I have a real sense of that?, W. wonders. Do I really know I am Max Brod rather than Franz Kafka? He doubts it, he says, which is why I never know the extent of my usurpation. For I am a usurper, says W.; I've stolen his place and the place of everyone. Who haven't I betrayed? What crime haven't I committed?

Still, says W., his burden is to take on my wrongdoings as though they were his own. It's all *his* fault, says W., even though it's all *my* fault. This is because he is certain he is Max Brod, while I still think I'm Franz Kafka.

You should never hang onto a conversation, says W. Once it's finished, *pfft*, it's finished. —'I forget everything you say as quickly as *that*', W. says, snapping his fingers in the air. I, on the contrary, remember everything, and not only that. —'You make things up', W. says. I wholly invent conversations we are supposed to have had, but in fact we never did have. I'm a fantastist, W. says, a dreamer, but for all that, I'm not without guilt. I'm no holy fool, W. says, no innocent. A fool, yes, but holy—not a bit of it.

I am neither an Eckermann nor a Boswell, W. says. I'm his ape, says W. and (remembering Benjamin's comment on Max Brod) a question mark in the margin of his life. Well, more like an exclamation mark, says W., or a shit stain.

Of course, W. never mistakes himself for Kafka, as I do. He's never thought himself anything other than a Max Brod. But the point is—this is W.'s first principle—the other person is always Kafka, which is why you should never write about them or hold on to their conversations, let alone make them up. Yes, the other person is always Kafka, W. says, even me. He knows that, says W., why don't I?

You have to know you're not Kafka, says W., that's the first thing. But you have to know that the person you're speaking to might be Kafka, that's the second. This is why conversation, for W., is always a matter for hope. The very ability to speak, to listen and respond, is already something, he says.

Of course, to speak to the other, to respond, is already to betray. Whatever you say is a betrayal, even if at the same time it is suffused with hope. That the other person might be

Kafka is a *perpetually present possibility*, says W. And that you are also the Brod who betrays Kafka is the *destruction* of this possibility, its disavowal.

In what sense is he Brod?, W. wonders. He knows the answer, he says. He never listens enough. He never gives himself over to what is being said. He always comes up short, says W., very short, which is why he always feels troubled when he speaks, yet at the same time always wants to push conversation towards the messianic.

'Even you', says W., 'even you might be Kafka, which would be a great miracle'. Of course, on the other hand, I'll never be Kafka *for myself*, but only for him, my conversationalist. The other person is never other *for himself*, says W. Or only rarely.

For haven't we along the way met thinkers—real thinkers —who speak without a concern for themselves, without any sense of self-preservation? It's as though what they say is indifferent to them, we agree. As though they are borne by thought, thought by it, rather than the other way round.

Yes, we have been fortunate to meet real thinkers, W. and I agree. It was our great good fortune. But wasn't it also our curse? Didn't we have confirmed for us that of which we would not be capable, that of which we *above all* would not be capable? It's important to know your limitations—on that we're agreed—but to have them reconfirmed so often; to have the sense of them closing around you like a cage?

We're being suffocated, we agree. How can we breathe? But an encounter with a real thinker is precisely that breath.

How is it possible, the sense that, with a thinker, a thought is shared between us? How is it possible that we believe ourselves to *participate in thinking*? Thought seems to occur between us. It seems to flow there, as though we were gathered around a mountain stream, around thought in its freshness, eternally streaming.

Ah to be near the source, at the beginning point! To have reached the highest, widest plateau with only the flashing stars above us! That's where these thinkers bring us; that's the vista their thought provides. Yes, we have seen the heights; thoughts, pure and fresh, have passed beside us.

Were we the condition of thought? We were only its occasion, alas. Someone spoke to us; we looked interested. Someone spoke; we listened. That was it. And thinking welled up around us like a great flood, and there were fishes in that flood, fish-thoughts streaming by us.

That was it, and nothing more. And with what were we left when the flood subsided? Where were we beached but on the valley-bottom of our stupidity, on the parched sands that no thought might cross?

W. sends me a quotation from his notebook:

For the youth of the world is past and the strength of creation already exhausted and the advent of times is very short. Yea, they have passed by, and the pitcher is near to the cistern and the ship to the port and the course of the journey to the city and life to its consummation.

It's from the Syriac *Book of Baruch*, a pseudo-epigraphic text from the period of the destruction of the temple, he says. Then he sends me another:

The world endlessly becomes itself, but because this process is endless the world never is the end towards which it moves. Similarly, God endlessly becomes himself by not being what the world has become, but because the world never becomes itself, neither does God become himself.

That's from Samuelson's *Judaism and the Doctrine of Creation*, W. says. It's meant to be an explanation of Rosenzweig's idea of creation. W. says I am endlessly failing to become what I am not. A thinker. A good person. A true friend.

Then he sends me a third, from Mascolo's *Le Communisme*, the greatest of all, he says, and to which he attaches no commentary:

One writes neither for the true proletarian, occupied elsewhere, and very well occupied, nor for the true bourgeois starved of goods, and who have not the ears. One writes for the disadjusted, neither proletarian nor bourgeois; that is to say, for one's friends, and less for the friends one has than for the innumerable unknown people who have the same life as us, who roughly and crudely understand the same things, are able to accept or must refuse the same, and who are in the same state of powerlessness and official silence.

Outside, half an inch of rendering now covers the back of the kitchen, I tell W. Today I placed my palm on its grey surface. Wet. Everything's wet, on both sides of the wall. Apparently there's a gap between two layers of brick. A gap—that's where the source of the damp is, I know it, I tell W. That's where it is: dark, wet matter without shape. Matter without light, as there is in dwarf galaxies stripped of gas.

And the damp's still spreading. There's still more of the wall to conquer. 'It'll be in your living room soon', says the damp expert. I nod. Yes, it will be everywhere. The flat will be made of damp, and spores will fill every part of the air. And I will breathe the spores and mould will flower inside me. And I'll live half in water, like a frog.

It is my own catastrophe, I tell W., it's very close to me.

A secret catastrophe, spreading from the gap between the layers of brick. I take people out there, to the kitchen, and run their hands along the wall. —'Feel it', I say, 'it's alive'. They're always impressed and disgusted.

W.'s book has come out, he says. His editor went down to dine with W. and brought him twenty copies of his own book. His editor proofread the manuscript several times and sent it out for proofreading. His book looks great, says W., except for the ancient Greek, which looks terrible. The Hebrew is okay, but the ancient Greek looks as though it were drawn by a child. It's hilarious.

His book is better than him, W. and I agree. It's greater. What's it about?, I ask him of a particularly difficult section. He's got no idea, he says. The book seems to stream splendidly above us both. Neither of us can follow it. Ah, the long example of his dog! It's even better than the sections on children in his previous book! W. says he's amazed too. How did he manage it?

I'm filling in my esteem indicators, I tell W. —'Oh yes, what are they?' He could do with a laugh, says W. 'How about humiliation indicators? Or soiling yourself indicators?', says W. 'Write about the history of your humiliations', says W. 'Write about dragging the rest of us down. Write about spoiling it for everyone, because that's what you've done'.

I hold my pen like an ape, W. has always observed, and no doubt I type like an ape too, my fingers slightly too large for the keys. And my book reads as though it were written by an ape, which is the worst thing of all, W. says.

'Once you were happy on your savannah', W. says. 'You were happy romping about with the whole horizon before you. What made you think you could read, let alone write? How did you end up mistaking yourself for a writer?

'Behold the idiot! That's what your book proclaims', says W. 'Wouldn't you like to go back to your savannah now? Wouldn't you like to hoot and romp with your fellow apes?'

Why do I write such bad books?, W. wonders. It's not even that they're bad at the level of content, which of course they are. The basics aren't even in place. The fundamentals. —'You can't write', says W. 'You're incapable of placing one word after another'.

Of course, my book was a lesson to him, W. says. His book, he decided, would be as good *at the level of style* as mine is bad, which is not to say it would be worthwhile *at the level of content*. But at least it would be legible, says

W. At least it would pass the minimum qualification for what would count as a book.

W.'s reading the notes he took ten years ago. —'They're better than anything I could do now', he says, sending me them. I agree: they are good. 'I had no girlfriend, barely any work, no television, and above all, no friend called Lars . . .' But didn't W. credit me with freeing him to write? Didn't I save him from years of writer's block? All I taught him was shamelessness, W. says. Compromise and half measures— that's all I taught him.

W. reminds me of the Hasidic lesson Scholem recounts towards the end of his great study of Jewish mysticism.

When he was confronted by a great task, the *first* Rabbi, about whom little is known—his name and the details of his life are shrouded in mystery—would go to a certain place in the woods, light a fire and meditate in prayer; and what he wanted to achieve was done.

A generation later, the *second* Rabbi—his name is not known, and only a few details have been passed down concerning his life—confronting a task of similar difficulty would go to the same place in the woods, and say, 'We can no longer light the fire, but we can still speak the prayers'. What he wanted to achieve was done.

Another generation passed, and the *third* Rabbi—whose name is known to us, but who remains, for all that, a legendary figure—went to the woods and said, 'We can no longer light the fire, nor do we know about the secret meditations belonging to the prayer. But we do know that place in the woods to which it all belongs—and that must be sufficient'. And what the Rabbi wanted to achieve was done.

Another generation passed, and perhaps others, who knows, and the *fourth* Rabbi—his name is well known, and he lived as we do—faced with a difficult task, merely sat in his armchair and said: 'We cannot light the fire, we cannot speak the prayers, we do not know the place, but we can tell the story of how it was done'. And that too was enough: what he wanted to achieve was done.

There was a *fifth* rabbi Scholem forgot—well, he wasn't really a rabbi, says W. His name is Lars, about whom all too much is known. He forgot where the woods were, and that he even had a task. His prayers, too, were forgotten; and if he meditated, it was upon the fate of Jordan and Peter André. He set fire to himself and his friend W. with his matches and the woods were burned to the ground. And then the whole world caught fire, the oceans boiled and the sky burned away and it was the end of days.

The washing powder has contracted into great wet lumps, I tell W. The salt is a single wet block. The sugar, the same. Where tins stand for an hour they leave a rusty mark. Dirt from the ceiling crumbles over everything. And it's so cold, so wet, the air full of spores. And salt covers the plaster like a beard. Salt in large flakes that you can rub away.

Leave kitchen roll standing for an hour and it's soaked. Leave a dry dishcloth on a worksurface and it's sodden. How wet is the air? Water condenses along the walls. And there are great green splodges where the mould is growing. You can't rub them away. They go deep: great, green splodges like nebulas.

I went out there again just now to remind myself, I tell W. Is it really that bad? It is that bad. Is it really that wet? Yes, it is that wet. Does dirt still fall from the ceiling? It falls, and constantly. I take a breath. Am I really breathing in spores? I'm breathing in spores. And I touch the wall above the sink—is something really running off on my hands? I look at them. There's something brown. Something wrong. There's a new process beginning on the wall, I tell W. Something horrible.

You can't be alone to experience the Messiah, W. says. Not really. And you can't be sober. The Messiah is drunk, says W. Or he's what drunkenness allows. Anyone can be the Messiah when he's drunk, W. says. Of course, he might not know it. W.'s not the Messiah *for himself*, W. says, just as I am not the Messiah *for myself*. He's the Messiah for me, and I'm the Messiah for him. Do I think of him, W., as the Messiah?, W. asks. Well, I should.

I am a sullen drinker, W. observes. Not for the whole evening, he admits—not even for most of it, but the time always comes when I refuse to say anything at all and slump down in my chair. —'That's when your immense belly becomes visible', says W., 'during the slump'. It's like Moby Dick, says W. Vast and white and rarely seen. But there it is in the slump. It always amazes him, says W. It amazes everyone.

I'm not like him, W. notes, for whom every conversation is on the verge of becoming messianic. W. likes to journey with his interlocutor through the apocalyptic and towards the messianic, he says. He believes in his interlocutor, not like me. He believes in conversation. I'm slumped, drunk and silent at one end of the table, W. says, while he is waiting for the Messiah at the other.

Anyone might be the Messiah, W. says. The Messiah might be me, says one Talmudic commentator. —'Are you the Messiah?', W. asks me. Is he? It's all to do with *the logic of relations*, W. says, his favourite topic. He is the Messiah for me just as I am the Messiah for him, not because of what each of us is for himself, but because of what we are for the other.

Is he the Messiah? Am I? The Messiah would never wear a shirt like that, W. says. He would never wear the trousers that are flapping round my ankles. The Messiah wouldn't buy his clothes from Primark, says W., he's sure of that.

Scholem says that there is a tradition of doubling the figure of the Messiah, W. tells me. The first Messiah belongs to the old world, and to the catastrophe that destroys the old world (messianism always entails catastrophe, W. observes). Every horror of the old world is concentrated in him. He can redeem nothing, and what can he desire but his own annihilation?

But then there is the Messiah ben David in whom all that is new announces itself, and who finally defeats the antichrist. He is the redeemer, W., says. He brings with him the messianic age.

Which one am I, do I think?, says W. Which one is he?

He can picture me, W. says, working at my desk, or attempting to work (or at least what I call work), covered in crumbs from the packed lunch I eat four hours early, surrounded by books by Schelling and Rosenzweig and Cohen, and by other books that explain Schelling and Rosenzweig and Cohen, and then by still other books with titles like *The Idiot's Guide to Jewish Messianism* and *Rosenzweig in Sixty Minutes*.

He can picture me, he says, hungover as usual, bleary-eyed as usual but full of a vague, stupid hope, with the sense that this time, despite its resemblance to all other times, will be different.

This time it'll be okay. This time it'll come good. That's my messianism, W. says, and it's all I'll ever know or understand about messianism, that vague sense that things will be different this time, even as everyone else knows they will be exactly the same.

'Even you feel it, don't you, that messianic hope? Even you, like the animals who come out of their burrows after winter, shivering but excited. But do you actually think you're going to be redeemed?'

W. himself can't shake it free, that hope, that springtime of the spirit. One day, he feels, he will be able to think. One day, his thoughts will rise as high as the Messiah, the sun in the sky of the future. Oh he knows it's impossible, he says, he knows he'll never have an idea, but that's what the coming of the Messiah must mean: the impossible, which is to say, an idea, an idea that would belong to W.

Is that why he writes?, W. wonders. Is that why he accepts invitations to speak? Is that why the hope is reborn eternally in him that it will be different this time? In the end, that's what we share, W. decides. A sense that the apocalypse isn't quite complete, and that there are still grounds for hope.

W. reminds me of the old story of the Messiah who remains hidden with the lepers and beggars at the gate of Rome. There he was all along; but is he there? When the Rabbi stands before him to ask when he will come, what does he say? *Today, if you will hear my voice.*

Today! Then the Messiah is here! But he is not here. There are conditions to his coming, and the leper-Messiah, who binds his wounds alongside the beggars at the gates of Rome, is not here yet.

There's a great lesson in this, W. says, though he's not sure what it is. When's the Messiah going to come? Today? Tomorrow? He's not sure, W. says, but it's only when you've exhausted everything, when there's no more hope, that the Messiah might appear.

Of course, I've long since worn W. out, he says. I'm hopeless, W. says. I'm unredeemable. W. knows it. But why then does he talk to me? Why does he continue with our collaboration?

Perhaps he hopes for something nonetheless, W. reflects. And perhaps it's only when he gives it up that the Messiah will arrive. Which would make me some kind of antichrist, W. surmises. A kind of living embodiment of the apocalypse.

The electrician came out, I tell W.—'It needs rewiring', he said, 'the whole flat'. I ignored him. There was light, and that was enough. The light in the kitchen is still working. It doesn't flicker; it's steady. Which means you can gaze upon the damp. You can gaze, fascinated, at the damp and the plaster mottled with damp. It doesn't hide, the damp. It isn't shy. It is there, obvious. It announces itself calmly. It says, *here I am*, with quiet plainness. And there it is, I tell W. A fact. Absolute damp. Damp beyond all damp meters. —'It's off the scale', said the drying expert who'll bring the machines.

Inside, in the kitchen, the damp continues to spread, but calmly, changing the colour of the wall. Along its spreading edges, thick salt falls to pile at the base of the wall and along the worksurfaces. Grit still falls from one corner of the ceiling. The wet walls are marked with mildew like liver spots on an elderly hand. And along the window sill, the plaster has turned a mottled green.

I have a small fan heater which I aim at this part of the wall, and then that, I tell W. Gradually, the plaster changes colour from an angry dark brown, mottled with dark green and black mould, to a calmer, lighter pink. It seems a miracle; it seems I'm winning, I tell W., how can this be? But then it comes back again, a wave of dark brown.

Periodically, I go out to the kitchen with some kitchen roll, and wipe down the great sweating surface. There's always a layer of water on the wall like a sweat sheen. I marvel. Is the wall alive? Does it live in some strange way? What is the meaning of the salt crystals which form on the wall? Is the salt the way it expresses itself, or dreams? Is it conscious and groping towards me to communicate? My flat is the satellite that turns around the damp, and I am the astronaut fascinated only by its changing surface.

Whole religions have formed around less, I tell W., around damp, and the source of damp.

W. sends me some quotations from the Talmud.

Seven things are hidden from men. These are the day of death, the day of consolation, the depth of judgement; no man knows what is in the mind of his friend; no man knows which of his business ventures will be profitable, or when the kingdom of the house of David will be restored, or when the sinful kingdom will fail.

W. likes lists, he says. It's a Borges thing. —'This quote is especially for you', he says:

Proselytes and those that emit semen to no purpose delay the Messiah.

'For how long have you personally delayed the coming of the Messiah?', says W. 'Years? Millennia?'

W. is sure he heard somewhere or another—at a lecture, symposium or suchlike—about the *stupid* Messiah, and this has oriented his research ever since. The stupid Messiah, whatever can that mean? When did this figure appear? Under what circumstances?

Of course, there is a long tradition of the *occultation* of the Messiah, W. says. The idea, that is, that the Messiah has already arrived, if only we could find him (if only we knew how to find him). Then there's the belief that it's only when certain *conditions* are satisfied that he will reveal himself to be where he always was. The moral improvement of humankind, for example.

But what could it mean to think of a Messiah so stupid that he is occulted from himself? Of a Messiah who does not have the intelligence to know he is the Messiah? There's a tradition, of course, that the Messiah would be the one who *broke* the law rather than simply fulfilling it. Whence the apostasy of Sabbatai Zevi, whose followers likewise committed apostasy, it being a sign for them of the kind of test the Messiah would ask them to undergo.

Would the stupid Messiah have stupid followers?, W. wonders. Followers so stupid they wouldn't know who they were following, or what it meant to follow? Mystery upon mystery, says W. But at least it goes some way to explaining my significance vis-à-vis messianism. Because I'm attracted to it, aren't I, in my own stupid way? Even I have a sense of the importance of the messianic idea as I circle around it in my stupidity.

W. is a little less unwitting than I, he says, a little less stupid. And perhaps that means I'm a truer follower of the stupid Messiah, he says, he's not certain.

Are we religious?, we wonder. I'm never quite sure. We feel things about religion, that's already something. There's an immense pathos about religious matters for us, that's certain. But are we religious, I mean *really* religious?

Wasn't it pathos that nearly made a Christian convert of Rosenzweig?, we wonder. Wasn't it the pathos of his friend Eugen Rosenstock, with whom he spent so many nights in conversation? There was one conversation in particular—that of the night of June 7th, 1913—which ended with Rosenzweig holding a pistol to his temple.

He had confronted the Nothing, he said later. He'd come to the very end. Rosenstock had persuaded him Judaism was outmoded, forgotten, and that Christianity was the only way redemption could be brought to the world. Rosenzweig agreed, but that wasn't what disturbed him. Asked what he would do when all the answers failed—when the abstract truths of logic failed to satisfy him—Rosenstock had said with great simplicity, *I would go to the next church, kneel and try to pray.*

Kneel and try to pray: that's what moved Rosenzweig, W. says. It moved him immeasurably, because those words came from a scholar, a thinker like him, not a naïf or a romantic. Forget the argument about redemption and Christianity and world history, it was *pathos* that brought about Rosenzweig's crisis, W. says. The pathos of a scholar who would live in faith and offer it as testimony.

Rosenzweig, of course, did not convert. Or rather, he converted back to Judaism. If he was to become Christian, he wrote to Rosenstock, it was to be *by way of Judaism*, W. says, even though his relationship to Judaism was weak. Even though his family was almost entirely assimilated.

But then a few days later, he attended the Yom Kippur service in an orthodox synagogue in Berlin. Up until that point, he felt one's relationship to God depended upon the mediation of Christ. And after it? Read *The Star*, and you'll see the Yom Kippur service is placed at the height of Rosenzweig's account of Jewish religious experience. At the height! Pathos again, says W. It's all about pathos.

Of course, there's pathos and pathos, W. says. What could we understand of Rosenzweig's despair after his conversion? How could we understand why he held a pistol to his temple, or what seeing the Nothing might mean?

Hadn't our second leader spoken to us at length of his faith? Hadn't we heard from his lips the testimony of one as far as possible from naivety or romanticism? But we were plunged into no crisis. We didn't contemplate our own deaths, or no more than usual. What did we feel? Stirred, moved to be sure, but it didn't translate into action.

Did we rush to a church and *kneel and try to pray*? Did we hold guns to our temples, or flail about in contemplation of the Nothing? Did we set about writing our own *Stars of Redemption*? Of course not. We fell short, says W., as we always fall short. But short of what? What idea could we have of faith, of the pathos of faith, as it streams infinitely far above our stupid heads?

'How depressed are you?', W. asks me on the phone. Very, I tell him. W.'s in his office in the southwest of the country, and I am in mine in the northeast. W. says he's looking out of the window and thinking of his failure. How has it come to this?, he thinks to himself over and over again.

Unopened parcels of review copies of books surround him, W. says. His office is thick with them. What can he do? I am the only person who would be interested in such books, W. says. They sicken him. They're like the ballast attached to a body to make sure it sinks, he says. And he is sinking.

It's different for me, W. acknowledges. I get some satisfaction from office work. It makes me think I've done something with my miserable life. It makes me feel my life is justified. W. can't bear it, though. Why does he go into work, then? What's the point? He could take a few days leave. But

W. feels something significant might happen in the office at any moment. He has to be there, W. says. Why? What will happen? He doesn't know, says W. Something momentous.

We're bottom feeders, W. says as he often does. We live on scraps. Soon there will be nothing for us, and then what? Well, the apocalypse will decide it all. It's coming, we agree. Our second leader told us so. In eight years time, wasn't it?, W. asks. Four years, I tell him. He's revised his estimate. —'Four years', says W. 'How will we survive until then? What will we do?' W. will be waiting in his office, the rain falling.

W. is still lost in Cohen, he says on the phone. What's it all about? He could be reading in Dutch for all he knows. Nevertheless, he sends me some notes for my edification, he says. This is what real scholarship is all about, he says.

I read. *Not the apparatus of knowledge itself, but in its outcomes, Ergebnis. Namely, science.* And a little later, *Unlike all the other fundamental concepts of Erkenntnistheorie, the concept of the infinitesimal does not have its roots in ancient thought.*

I'm impressed, I tell W. —'You're always impressed!', W. says. 'Anything could impress you, monkey boy'.

W. says he can only stand reading Cohen for two hours a day. Two hours, from dawn to six A.M, then up for breakfast and into the office. He never understands a word, not really.

W.'s come to the chapter on conic sections, he says. Do you know what a conic section is?, he asks me. It's a transverse section through a cone, I tell him. It's something to do with Kepler. Now it's W.'s turn to be impressed. I have odd corners of knowledge, he says. Like the German for badger, for example—what was it? *Der Dachs,* I told him, that's why you get dachshunds.

Anyway, W. says, there are three types of conic section: hyperbolic, parabolic and the other one—it isn't anything -*bolic*, it's just normal. —'I think that's what it's called: normal', W. says. 'Anyway, which one are you: hyperbolic or parabolic? Do you view yourself as a hyperbolic man or a parabolic man?'

Sometimes, W. dreams we will become mathematical thinkers, I the philosopher of infinitesimal calculus, he the philosopher of conic sections.

Mathematics is the organon, says W. pedagogically. Do you know what organon means? He didn't know himself, W. says. It comes from Aristotle, and refers to an overall conceptual system—the categories and so on.

W. is growing increasingly certain that the route to religion is a mathematical one. Maths, that's what it's all about. Take Cohen, for example. And Rosenzweig. Of course no one can understand Rosenzweig on mathematics and religion, W. says.

For his part, W.'s been reading his Hebrew Bible again, and wondering how to *mathematise* it. He's quite serious, he says. He is currently in an email exchange on the topic with one of his cleverer friends, he says.

The infinitesimally small is not a concept of thought, but of science, and the science of magnitudes, Groessen. But does not the idea of magnitude presuppose intuition? Thus there appears to be a contradiction between thought and intuition. How can the infinitesimal be a magnitude and at the same time not an intuition?

W. says he's since discovered that *Groessen*, in the last paragraph, can also be translated *dimension*. He's not sure what the implications of that might be, though.

Has he had a thought over the weekend?, I ask W. No, he says, not one. He never thinks when he's with me. But I think sometimes, W. notes, sometimes I'm capable of thought. There's sometimes a parting of the clouds, it's amazing. For a few minutes, I make sense, I speak clearly and thoughtfully, and everyone is amazed. Sal was impressed at Oxford, says W., remembering our conversation in the beer garden. Ah yes, the beer garden, I say, a moment of illumination.

The problem is that I fear time, W. has decided. I have no stretches of empty time in my day. W., by contrast, always allows for empty time in his day. When he eats, he eats, he doesn't work. When I eat, by contrast, it is in front of the computer screen, crumbs dropping between the keys. —'What time do you get up?', says W., wanting to be taken through my work day. At six o'clock, I tell him. He gets up at *four*, he

says, sometimes earlier. I got up at five yesterday, I tell him.
—'And what did you do?' I wrote, I tell him. —'But did you
think?', W. asks. 'You can't think *and* write'.

Yes, my problem is that I fear empty time, W. is sure of
it. Does he fear it? No, he says, but then his house is nicer
than my flat. And his living room walls aren't pink. —'What
were you thinking when you painted those walls?' It was to
bring out the colour of the wood, I tell him. Pink, though!
Why pink? It would depress him, says W.

'So what are you going to do about your leak?', says W.
I show him the kitchen. The dehumidifiers, working twenty-
four hours a day, are sucking out the damp. They fill up every
twelve hours. —'That's a lot of water', says W. 'Where does
it come from?' No one knows, I tell him. The greatest experts
on damp are completely baffled.

W. wants to understand me, he says. He's decided to list my
affects. You can do it for any living thing, he says. A tick, for
example, responds to heat and warmth. —'It's a very simple
being. Like you. You're simple'.

'We'll start with the living room', he says. Am I taking
notes? I'm writing on a post-it pad. —'It's cold', he says.
'Write that down. I'm freezing. How can you live like this?
And it's dark', he says. 'There's no light. I can't see anything.
And it's damp. That's another affect'. It's better than it was,
I tell him.

Why am I always putting vaseline on my lips?, W.

wonders. —'Vaseline', he says, that's another of your affects. The internet. That's what scholarship is for you, isn't it? How can you go on reading that bilge? You've got no honour. No shame. No goodness'.

W. looks out of the window at the rotting plants in the yard. —'Horror. That's your other affect, isn't it? Look at it out there. It's shit. How can you live like this?'

W. is delineating the basic categories, he says. —'Television. You like TV, don't you?', says W. I tell him I don't watch it that much. —'I'm not surprised. The remote is broken. How can you watch anything?'

'So what else do you do? Are there any affects for you in the bathroom?' I'm indifferent to the bathroom, I tell him. —'What do you think about when you're in there?' Nothing, I tell him. You, I tell him, and he laughs.

'Well then, your bedroom. Is that where you do your reading? You don't really read anything, do you? You don't read. And what about the kitchen? Those stacks of tinned fish. You eat the same thing every day, don't you? Exactly the same thing!' W. is a believer in a varied diet, he says. —'I try to vary what I eat. Not like you'.

W. concludes he has a larger range of affects than me. He lives with someone. That's what does it. —'Otherwise I'd be a sad fucker like you'. Of course W.'s house is much nicer, he points out. It's not cold, for one thing. Or dark. Or damp.

The previous owners dug right down to the foundations to get rid of the damp, W. tells me. They put down a layer of plastic sheeting, then a layer of concrete, then another layer of sheeting, all the way up. —'It's dry as a bone', W. says.

W.'s tired of listing my affects. How many have we got?

Eight general categories, I tell him. He looks around. —'Oh fuck it, that will do'.

W. feels ill from all the drinking, he says. Last night, we had a bottle of red wine, then beer, then we drank Tequila from the bottle. Then we finished off the bottle of Plymouth Gin, then a bottle of Cava and then a bottle of Chablis. It was a good Chablis, wasn't it? W. says he was in no position to appreciate it. He wants some aspirin, he says. —'And how are you feeling?', he asks me. Fine, I tell him. Better than usual. —'Any thoughts?' Not one.

We head out to the coast for the day, and eat fish and chips on the Fish Quay. We wander through the deserted markets. It's a melancholy sight. There's a special kind of melancholy to the quayside, W. and I agree. What is it? The sense that it's all over, it's all finished, and a whole civilisation has come to an end, which in fact it has.

We watch the big seagulls strutting about, and the pigeons. —'What do you feel about pigeons?', W. asks me. The Romans brought them to England to eat. They crowd on his window ledge every morning, W. says, cooing and flapping their wings. What miserable birds! He prefers the seagulls, of course. They remind him of the sea, he says, and he loves the sea.

On one side of us, the Tyne broadens as it reaches its end; on the other, a passenger ferry at the dock, ready to disembark for Norway. Should we go to Norway?, W, wonders. Would they make sense of us there?

'Your problem is that you fear empty time', says W.

as we head back to the city. 'That's why you don't think'. And then: 'Thought must come as a surprise, when you least expect it'.

Thought, when it comes, always surprises him, says W. But he's ready with his notebook, he says, which he keeps in his man bag. That's why I need a man bag, he says, in case thought surprises me. But I fear the empty time which makes thought possible, says W., so I don't need a man bag.

The next morning, W.'s flight is cancelled. He's stranded in my flat for another day and night. This place is a shithole, he says, and starts to read Spinoza to forget the cold and the dark and the damp.

When he reads Spinoza, W. says, he feels beatitude. Beatitude, he says, the third level of knowledge. —'You've never felt beatitude', says W. 'You're not capable of it'.

W. is a mystic. One day he might become properly religious. —'Do you think you'll ever become religious?', he asks me. He says that he might. Sometimes he feels on the verge of religion.

W. says *The Ethics* is the only book he's ever thought is completely right. —'It's the opposite of your flat', says W. 'God, it's cold. And dark. Why is it so dark? And why does nothing work? Half your lights, for example. Your kitchen. Your TV. Do you just go into the shops and ask for the shittiest thing they have?', says W. 'Nothing ever changes for you, does it? There's no movement forward'.

W. wants to read Spinoza in Latin, but he's forgotten all he knew of the language. He'll have to learn it again! But it's not a chore. —'You have to read in the original language', he says. 'Of course you wouldn't know anything about that'. Next he'll refresh his Greek.

W. recalls our Greek lessons, he on sabbatical, me a young student. —'You seemed intelligent then, full of promise'. Of course, I was no such thing, he realised quickly. W. and the others had the answer book and used to crib from its translations in advance. They liked to watch me squirm with my exercises. —'Your idiocy was spectacular', says W. '*Omoi!*, that's was all you could say. *Omoi!*, *omoi!*, like a wounded bull'.

For his part, W. has given up learning differential calculus. —'It's beyond me', he says. Will he ever really understand Leibniz—or Cohen, with his mathematical mysticism? Never mind, he says; he has Spinoza. —'Ah, *The Ethics*', he sighs. 'Beatitude!', he sighs.

The damp, I say to W. That's my apocalypse. Does he know I have mushrooms growing from the ceiling? Does he know they're gathered in the far upper corner of the kitchen? It used to make me shudder, I tell W. I used to hate it. But now . . .

I'm fascinated by the damp, I tell W. I can't help it. I go out there again, to the kitchen, to the bathroom. I put my hand on the clammy wall. The damp is calling me. The damp wants a witness to itself. And who am I but the one who sees it, touches it? Who am I but the one with its spores in his lungs?

One night it grew me, I tell W. One night a spore unfolded itself to a make a man, a golem of damp. And the damp wrote its name on my forehead and placed its charm on my tongue . . .

Somewhere, on the other side of the wall, life has reached

a new level, I tell W. Somewhere, damp mutters to itself; damp dreams, there behind the wall. And what will it say when it comes to itself? What will it say when it wakes up?

What will he write about next?, W. muses. What's to be his next project? He's casting about, he admits it. Wasn't he supposed to learn Greek this summer? Protestant guilt keeps driving him into the office, he says. In he goes on the bus, thinking he ought to be doing something, but not quite sure what. He sits in the office among the parcels of review copies of books he keeps receiving. There are dozens of them, piled up all over the place. They depress him enormously. He can't bear to look at them.

For my part, W. notes, I still have a stupid excitement about books. It's because I'm illiterate, W. says, and because they're slightly above the level I can understand. Whenever I visit, I insist on opening the parcels and filling up W.'s shelves with fresh new books, reading him the most ridiculous of the blurbs. It must be the bright covers that attract me, W. says, whereas they depress him horribly. —'All these books!', he says, with weary horror. 'Look at them!'

Whatever happened to W.'s publisher? Once the most gener-ous and gregarious of men, he insisted upon travelling hun-dreds of miles to visit W. and take him out to dinner. They spent days going over the manuscript, which was properly proofread (not like mine, W. says, which was farmed out to Malaysia). And he'd decided on a full colour cover for the paperback—an expensive undertaking, W. notes. Granted, the final version still had typos on the first page (to his amuse-ment) and even in the blurbs on the back (which he found even funnier), but it was a handsome volume, and one of a series of handsome volumes.

But what's happened to the publisher? He's gone out of business, that much is clear. Of course, you could never get hold of his books anywhere, which also amused W. As soon as his book was in print, it was out of print, he said. It was always and already out of print, he said, which was fitting, he said. Luckily, he got a box of free copies, says W., which he sent to his friends. Were it not for that, no one would believe it had existed.

To W., it's completely inconsequential whether the book is in print or not. You should always publish with friends, he says, and the publisher was a friend. But where is he? He doesn't reply to emails or telephone calls, W. says. Doubtless there's no longer a computer in his office, nor a telephone, he says. Doubtless the office has long been stripped and demol-ished, and he's sitting sobbing in the ruins.

You should always publish with friends, W. notes, and that's all he wants from his vanished publisher: a sign of friendship, of their shared failure. That's all he would want from any of his friends, who are all failures, whether they know it or not.

Why has everything become so absurd?, I ask W. Why has it all come apart just at the moment when we might have got somewhere? But W. reminds me of what we both know: that any success we've had is premised upon exactly that absurdity.

We're like captains of the Titanic, we tell each other. W.'s already steered his ship into the iceberg. It's wrecked— all hands lost. W. remains on the bridge, the last man standing, but there's not long left. —'It'll be your turn next', says W. 'How long do you think you'll last?'

The iceberg's looming, I tell W. I'm mesmerised by it. So was he, says W. He knew it was coming and that it could only come. He knew that any success he had had was premised upon this greater and pre-ordained failure. He's dignified in defeat. —'Not like you', he says, 'gnashing your teeth and wailing from the rooftops'.

I am getting to know the moods of the damp, I tell W. The kitchen walls, still bare, sometimes seem to glower with anger: they become darker, browner. And then, at other times, they seem to lighten: the damp is in a good mood, or it has been dreamily distracted from the work of dampening. Is it a god that needs to be appeased, and if so, with what kind of sacrifice? But if it is a god, or part of a god, it is an inscrutable one; I follow its moods without being able to understand them.

Sometimes it darkens, it becomes browner, as though gathering itself up. Particularly, high up the wall, like a dark cloud spread all along—the damp becomes more intense. But it is not quite wet, not anymore. The surface is smooth, but not really moist; and it's not running with water as it used to be. Dehumidifiers work night and day in the kitchen. Night and day, and though pinpricks of damp appear where there was once white plaster, dried out by the heater, the wall never grows wetter. Has the damp been conquered, or only contained?

The damp and I are companions in the quiet flat. Little happens here; the damp does its work as moisture is drawn through the filters of the dehumidifier into its transparent collection tray, and I try to do mine. When I am away, I tell W., I think the damp plunges forward like a dark wave; I can smell it, very thick in the air, when I open the door. Damp in a wave, welcoming me home, thick and brown and wet in the air.

Sometimes I sponge down the walls with a mixture of water and bleach. It needs to be done in the bathroom, too, where black spores of mould are forming. And the wallpaper in the bedroom, too. But these are only symptoms. I touch a cool sponge to the wall as to a fevered brow. Be calm, be still, do not toss and turn. And now I imagine the damp is a dream of the wall, that it is lost in itself somehow, and that if the wall were only to open its eyes and see me, then all would be well. But the wall seems to fall into itself. It's lost in damp, or damp is what rises up when the wall disappears into its coma.

Sometimes, I tell W., I like to imagine that I could pick the walls up like a Chinese screen and turn them to the sun to dry. To lift up the ceiling and the flat above and let the sun find the wall, and dry it. That would let it live. That would awaken it. As it is, the wall is hunched upon itself and hidden from the sun. It weeps in a corner.

But how long for? I think warmer days are approaching, I tell W., though it was freezing today, and there were a few snowflakes in the air. Warmer days, and the simple honesty of the sun, which will bake everything dry. And if I cannot pick up the wall to turn it around, inner to outer, so there are no secrets anymore, nothing hidden, there is still the slow penetration of the sun, slow, and over the whole outer wall, rendered and unrendered. And one day it will be summer, too, in my kitchen.

The disaster has already happened, said W. during our presentation. That's what we're committed to, he said, meaning him and me. It's already happened! It's all finished! Can't you see that it's finished? But no one agreed with us. We're quite alone, we agreed afterwards, walking to the train.

Alone with the apocalypse! The only thing for it is to drink. Luckily we have a bottle of Plymouth Gin in our bag. We are sober men, terribly sober, we agree. It's only those who are the most sober of all who have to drink, and then to the point when they can no longer pronounce the word *apocalypse*. It's only then, drunk as lords, that they will know God's plan, which they will immediately forget.

Are we capable of religious belief? Of course not. We're not capable of anything, that's the trouble. We're up against the apocalypse with no means to fight it. *The disaster has already happened.* We were born, for one thing. We're going to die, that's another. And the oceans will boil and the skies burn away into the outer darkness . . .

It's all over, it's all finished. This is the interregnum. A little reprieve, an Indian summer. But we're deep into autumn, and winter is coming—or should that be the other way round? Deep into spring—a new kind of spring, a boiling spring—and a summer will come that will burn away everything.

Maybe it will come later, after we're dead. Maybe sooner—tomorrow, or the day after tomorrow. But in another sense, it's already come; it's spread its cloak around us. We're men of the End, of the Very End. We're men of the Disaster, which no one else knows but us. Which no one else *feels.* Drink, drink, we have to drink. We unscrew the top of our gin bottle as the train rolls out of the station . . .

These are the End Times, but who knows it but us? No one. We're quite alone with our knowledge, which is really a kind of feeling. We're on our own, we decide. That's what we have in common: a sense of the apocalypse. A sense that the time has come, and these are the days of our Judgement.

We'll be found wanting, we know that. We two above all—we're terribly guilty. What's to become of us—of us in particular? No one believes in us. No one listens. We're out on a limb—terribly far—and we're sawing it off. We'll fall off the edge of the world. We are falling—who believes us? Who believes in us?

These are our thoughts on the train that rushes through

the night. We're drinking gin with great determination. We have to drink!, drink! until we can no longer say the word, *Messiah*. That's our punishment, and we must be punished. This is what it has come to, here in the dark, rushing forward . . .

What place do we have in the world? None. Where's it all going? To perdition. To desolation, and to the abomination of desolation. And are we going with it? All the way! That's where we're heading now with our gin and our apocalypticism, full speed into the night.

Messianism has driven us mad, or half mad, we decide. What else have we been thinking about? What else has driven us through our reading and writing? We'll be glad when it's over: but when will it be over? There's no sign yet. Messianism hasn't finished with us.

We're fated in some way. We're circling round and round what we cannot possibly understand. And isn't that why we're drawn to it? Isn't that the lure? You cannot understand this idea. You'll never understand it, not today, not tomorrow. But the day after that?, we ask. The day after tomorrow?

That's our faith: it's not faith in the Messiah, but that we might be brought into the vicinity of the *idea* of the Messiah; that a little of its light might reach us. The Messiah: isn't he forever beyond us, just beyond? We've always just missed him. We missed the appointment . . .

Wasn't he supposed to arrive here, now? Not today, and not even tomorrow. But the *idea* of the Messiah: might we reach that? Is there something left of his passing, some trace—some sign? The day after tomorrow: that's when it will reach us, if it does: the *idea* of the Messiah.

But won't it have been too late? Won't the page have already been turned? But perhaps that's what it means: the idea can burn only for those who cannot see it, who have already gone under. It's on the other side of the mirror, although all they can see are their own stupid faces.

And what do we see, in the reflective surface of the train windows? Whose faces are those behind the glass? —'My God, look at us', says W. 'Look what we've become'.

The water taxi to Mount Batten. We're in choppy water, but sit out nevertheless on the exposed part of the deck. —'Poseidon must be angry', says W. as the surf splashes over us. W.'s learning Greek again. Is it the fifth time he's begun? The sixth? It's the aorist that defeats him, he says. Every time.

It's choppy! —'We should libate the sea', says W. Then he asks me if I know why the sea is salty. It's because the mountains are salty and the sea is full of broken up mountains, he says.

It's also full of ozone, of course. That's what cheers you up when you're near the sea, W. says, the ozone that choppy water releases into the air.

Have we failed? W. is certain: we are complete failures. We

should be drowned like kittens, he says, for the little we've achieved. But what chance did we have?, I ask him. What could we have done, under the circumstances? That's always my question, W. says. —'You're always looking for excuses. It's your Hindu fatalism'.

W. says my entire worldview is organised so that I never have to take responsibility for anything, even my supposed Hinduism. W. was brought up with the idea of eternal damnation, he says, and the thought of it still makes him shiver. Hindus are immune, W. says. I should try living as a Catholic and then I'd see (W.'s family were converts, of course). And as a Jew (W. is Jewish by bloodline). —'It's the guilt that's worst', says W. 'The sense you can never measure up'.

'Detachment, that's what you Hindus have to achieve to escape the wheel of rebirth, isn't it?', W. says. *Moksha*: the cessation of desire. It makes sense to him, W. says. Look at my flat, for one thing. It's disgusting. Do I desire to clean it up? No. Do I desire to deal with the damp? Not really.

'It's a kind of test for you, isn't it, your damp?' W. says. All I have to do is to desire not to change it, W. says. All I would have to say is, *The damp is eternal; I accept that now.* That would be *moksha*, wouldn't it? Ah, if only it were as simple for him, W. says.

'This is how proper people think', says W. in the beer garden in Turnchapel, his arms held behind his back and his head raised. 'Do I look as though I'm having lofty thoughts?'

What thoughts has he had? I read from the back of his notebook. *The messianic and the apocalyptic*, it says, the 'and' underlined. *Pathos*, it says. *Blood in the chinks between the stones of the law—Kafka*, it says. *Groessen = dimension*, it says. *Capitalism = paganism*. And then, *The real future is waiting to happen beneath the marketing of the future.*

And then, a little further on: *We have to live two lives, one turned to the world and to the horror of the world, and the other turned to our friends*. And still further on, *Eternity in time*. And then, *Kafka—thin, Brod—fat.*

There's a list of ingredients, too: *juniper (Italy), lemon and orange peel (Spain), orris root (Italy), Angelica root (Low Countries), cardamom pods (Sri Lanka), coriander seeds (Russia)*. And some tasting records: *Warm spiciness. Peppery notes. Earthiness and sweetness*. That was from the visit of the Chief Distiller of Plymouth Gin, W. says.

W. cherishes my special love for Turnchapel. I become gentler when I'm there, he notes, kinder. He likes my tender side. In another life, I could have lived here, imagine . . . We muse wistfully on what I might have been like. —'A better person', W. thinks, 'taller, with some nobility of character'.

In the staff dining room, framed portraits of VCs in their robes all around us, W. confides that he thinks he's on the brink of an idea. He's never had an idea before, so he doesn't quite know what it's like. But he thinks this is it: he's on the brink of an idea; a new horizon is opening before him. Have I ever had an idea?, he asks. Of course not, he says, why is he asking? Have I ever thought I was on the *brink* of an idea, and that people would haul me up on their shoulders and carry me around, cheering?

'Of course you never thought you'd have an idea for a moment, did you?', W. says. 'You actually *repel* ideas and intelligent thought', W. says. 'Never for a moment would you be capable of thinking', W. says. 'Not for one moment!'

When he was young, W. was sure that one day, if he worked hard enough, he'd have an idea. He lodged in an attic room in which there was only a bed and a work table. A bed and a desk, W. emphasises. He rarely left it, his attic room, W. says. He worked night and day. Reading and writing were all that mattered.

What happened? Ah, we know what happened! He's told me a million times! He's told everyone! He discovered drinking, says W., and smoking! He came late to both, but when he discovered drinking and smoking that was it! But no doubt he began drinking and smoking from a sense of disappointment, from the knowledge he'd never have an idea and that there was no point in going on, he says. Yes, that's what happened, W. says: disappointment, and then drinking (and smoking). Then there was the apocalypse, which made things even worse.

Since then, he's lived in the ruins of his impression of himself as someone capable of having ideas. He's felt ill for years, says W., which, on top of his drinking and general disappointment may have prevented him from having an idea (until now), or be the result of him not having an idea (until now). But W. thinks he may be at the beginnings of an idea. At its rudiments, he says.

W. points out a strip of trees from the window, which looks towards Plymouth and the sea. It's ancient woodland, he tells me. That's all that's left of it, that strip, he says, which runs right up to Dartmoor. There's a species of tree, unique to the area, that grows there: the Plym pear, he says. You can't eat the pears, though, they're like crabapples.

Why has he brought me up here? Why this vista from the staffroom window all the way towards the glistening sea? —'Infinite judgement', he says, mysteriously. 'That's my idea.

Infinite—judgement. It's from Cohen', he says. 'Well, it's from Cohen's reading of Kant'.

W. has been sending me his notes on Cohen for months. He barely understands a word of Cohen, W. has always admitted. In fact, he is singularly unqualified to read Cohen, lacking any understanding of mathematics, which is essential, or any real religious feeling.

Infinite judgement. Whatever does it mean? W.'s not sure, but nevertheless he feels he's on to something. He's not sure, he says, whether he has made a genuine breakthrough, or whether it is all nonsense. Is he at the summit of his creativity or the peak of his idiocy?

At the bus-stop by the hospital, W. shows me the dedication of the book he's recently added to his collection. *To my Rabbi* . . . It's dedicated to his Rabbi, says W., wonderingly. W. has always wished he had a Rabbi to whom to dedicate his books. Or rather, he now knows that that is what he should have wished for all along.

A Rabbi! He would have been part of something. He would have had a sense of belonging. Despite his interest in Jewish topics, W. is not really a Jew. He's not even a Catholic, not really, W. says. He's not capable of believing in anything, not anymore. There's no-one more boring than an atheist, W. sighs.

Of course he looks very Jewish, W. says, especially since he's grown his hair long. But however Talmudic he appears (and he has looked increasingly Talmudic in recent years, with his beard and long ringlets), there is the terrible reality of his non-belief.

As we cross Mutley Plain, looking out of the window of the bus, W. speaks of his obsession with the great Hungarian plain. Béla Tarr spent six months visiting every house and every pub on the plain, W. notes. He said he discovered mud, rain and the infinite, in that order. *Mud, rain and the infinite*: nothing to W. is more moving than those words.

W. wonders whether we too have discovered the infinite in our own way. Our incessant chatter. Our incessant feeling of utter failure. Perhaps we live on our own version of the plain, W. muses. Am I the plain on which he is lost, or vice versa? But perhaps the plain is the friendship between us on which we are both lost, he says.